"I didn't have time for a fancy plan," Daisy said.

"I've got a gun. I've got my martial arts training. I figured I'll come up with some genius move on the fly."

Ah, the Daisy Lopez bravado. Sometimes it got her out of jams. Sometimes it made things worse.

"Well, now that you've got me here to help, what's the new plan?" Martin asked.

"Once my mom's in the clear and they're holding on to me instead of her, we take them down. You pop out of the SUV. They'll be surprised. I pull out my gun and take on whoever is on my right. You take the other one."

A highly risky plan, but they were backed into a corner right now with few options.

Daisy's phone chimed. "No," she muttered. And then much more forcefully she said, "No, no, *no.*"

Martin's gut clenched. Something was obviously wrong. "What's happening?"

"I got a text from the thugs we're chasing. They want to do the exchange in a different location."

Martin's heart sank. A last-minute change made the situation more unpredictable. And much more dangerous.

Jenna Night comes from a family of Southern-born natural storytellers. Her parents were avid readers and the house was always filled with books. No wonder she grew up wanting to tell her own stories. She's lived on both coasts but currently resides in the Inland Northwest, where she's astonished by the occasional glimpse of a moose, a herd of elk or a soaring eagle.

Visit the Author Profile page at Harlequin.com.

HOSTAGE PURSUIT

JENNA NIGHT

LOVE INSPIRED SUSPENSE
INSPIRATIONAL ROMANCE

LOVE INSPIRED® SUSPENSE

INSPIRATIONAL ROMANCE

ISBN-13: 978-1-335-40504-3

Please Recycle. This product is recyclable.

Recycling programs for this product may not exist in your area.

Hostage Pursuit

This edition published by arrangement with Harlequin Books S.A.

For questions and comments about the quality of this book, please contact us at CustomerService@Harlequin.com.

Love Inspired
22 Adelaide St. West, 40th Floor
Toronto, Ontario M5H 4E3, Canada
www.Harlequin.com

Printed in U.S.A.

Many sorrows shall be to the wicked; but he that
trusteth in the Lord, mercy shall compass him about.
−Psalm 32:10

To my mom, Esther.

ONE

"They've got my mom. They say they'll kill her if I call the police."

Bounty hunter Daisy Lopez felt her breath catch in her throat as she stopped dead in her tracks and read the threatening text on her phone. Her heart hammered so furiously in her chest that it seemed as if her lungs wouldn't work. And her stomach suddenly felt like a twisted block of ice. She tore her gaze away from the words and held out her phone with the screen facing her boss and fellow bounty hunter, Alvis Carter, so that he could see the message.

"This is no idle threat," she added, the tension in her tightened throat making the words come out as a distraught whisper. "They *really will* kill her."

Alvis sighed and nodded. "You're right." Sunlight filtered through the pines surrounding the dirt parking lot where they were standing and shone down on the gray stubble covering his upper lip and chin. Alvis was still mentally a sharp tracker, but he'd reached a point in life where the physical side of the job took a toll on him pretty quickly. That meant he counted on Daisy to do most of the running and climbing when they were chasing bad guys, which was fine with her. "What do you want to do?" he asked.

That was a good question.

At the moment they were on the trail of a pair of mob-connected professional hit men trying to escape the long arm of the law out of Miami by hiding in Jameson, Montana. Daisy had started the hunt for the bail jumpers five days ago, showing photos of Beau Daltrey and Ivan Bunker to people at hotels, gas stations and restaurants, and to Realtors who specialized in short-term rental properties. Alvis had finished up another case he'd been working and had joined in Daisy's chase this morning. They'd just left a realty office where an employee had looked at photos and confirmed that she'd seen Daltrey and Bunker when the text announcing the abduction of Shannon Lopez arrived on Daisy's phone. Clearly, the Miami mob assassins had figured out that Daisy was hot on their trail.

She and Alvis resumed walking toward her SUV when her phone chimed again with a text message from the same unknown number.

She tapped on the message and was once more stopped in her tracks when she saw the horrifying video image that opened on the screen. It was her mother, with her hands and feet bound with duct tape and a strip of cloth tied across her mouth. Her eyes were huge and filled with terror.

A voice off camera started to speak and Daisy quickly increased the volume. "Stop looking for us," a man said. "When we get far enough away, we'll set your mother free. Until then, back off. If you call the cops, she dies."

Daisy's entire body was shaking by the time the short message ended. She played it three more times, with Alvis coming around behind her to peer over her shoulder and watch it with her. It took several seconds after the last viewing before she could take a step. Her body was numb and it felt like her feet were encased in concrete. She barely made it to her SUV, where she dropped into the driver's seat as a cold wave of terror slammed through her.

"This is bad," Alvis said, his voice husky with emotion. "I know they said not to do it, but maybe getting law enforcement involved is the best call."

Daisy met his gaze and she saw the sorrow and defeat in his eyes. He was probably thinking the same thing she was. That the two hit men would likely kill Shannon no matter what Daisy did. They had nothing to lose. They were already facing murder charges back in Miami and they were obviously desperate to stay out of prison.

But this was Daisy's *mom*. She couldn't give up on her. There had to be something she could do. She watched the video again, this time forcing herself to shove her emotions aside and focus on what she could see. Because in the middle of her heartbreak and horror while viewing the video the previous times, her brain had registered the sight of something familiar.

"Are you seeing what I'm seeing?" she asked Alvis, tilting her phone slightly to give him a better view.

"Yeah," he said slowly. "That looks like the Jameson Recreation Hall on the east side of Lake Dillon."

The video focused mainly on Shannon lying tied up in the back of the SUV with the hatch open. But several yards away was a section of a wooden structure that looked familiar. Daisy couldn't see the whole thing, but it appeared to be a segment of the L-shaped building with dining facilities and an area where paddleboards and other pieces of sports equipment were rented out in the warmer summer months. Now that it was early October and already dropping to near-freezing temperatures at night, the building would be closed up for the season.

Daisy started the engine of her SUV. "They might not still be there, but let's go have a look. I don't want to call the police yet. The last thing we need is an officer in a patrol car up there looking around. That could spook Daltrey and Bunker, and if they have to make a quick escape, they might decide that dragging my mom along with them is too much trouble." She swallowed thickly. "They might decide they don't want to leave a witness behind who could help the cops find them. They might shoot her."

Daisy gripped the steering wheel so tightly that her knuckles were white as she drove to the recreation hall as fast as she could, hoping and praying that the fugitives from Miami didn't realize how easily identifiable the building was to someone who'd lived in Jameson all her life.

As they crested the rise just before the lake came into view, she took a deep breath and forced herself to slow down so she'd look like a typical citizen out for a drive. There was no telling if the bad guys were watching.

She continued along the road as it hugged the edge

of the lake, driving as close to the recreation hall as she dared and then pulling off to the side and parking under the cover of the pine forest. She slid out of the SUV, her hands and knees still shaking from the surge of adrenaline that nearly had her heart bursting out of her chest with worry for her mom, and crept forward until she found a good vantage point. Alvis stayed close behind her.

There was an SUV in the parking lot. It matched the one in the video. They might have just abandoned the vehicle here. Or they might actually be inside the building *with her mom*.

It made sense that the fugitives hadn't gone far. Ditching Shannon somewhere and sneaking out through the regional airport wasn't an option. Federal authorities had been alerted to be on the lookout for them for a while now. And even though Jameson was a good-sized town by Montana standards and home to Dawson University, it was also surrounded by miles and miles of rough terrain and very few roads. Since the fugitives were still driving the same SUV shown in the video, if Daisy had contacted the police and the hit men had tried to jackrabbit out of town, the Montana Highway Patrol would have easily intercepted them. The bad guys must have decided to stay put for a while until they were certain they had achieved their goal by kidnapping Shannon and that Daisy had stopped hunting them.

"Time to call the cops and wait for them to arrive," Alvis said.

"Agreed." The panic that had been radiating from her chest up into her throat finally subsided enough that Daisy could take a deep breath. She had to keep herself together if she was going to help get her mother out of this situation alive. The bail-jumping fugitives who had taken Shannon had killed before. They wouldn't hesitate to kill again.

Daisy took another deep breath and silently said a quick prayer for guidance.

"Okay," she said to Alvis. "Call it in. And while we're waiting for the cops to arrive, I'll go over and disable their SUV so they can't get away." She grabbed a multipurpose knife from the glove box, and then pulled her phone from her pocket and completely silenced it. It was quiet by the mountain lake, with only the slight sounds of the breeze rustling the tops of the trees and the water lapping against the lakeshore. She didn't want sounds coming from her phone to alert the bad guys that she was there.

"I'll go with you," Alvis said.

"No. Stay back here where you've got a good overview of the area. Text me if anything happens that I need to know about. I won't hear the notification, but I'll make sure I glance at the screen a few times. Be right back."

She scurried through the forest to the edge of the gravel parking lot, where she was forced to break cover to traverse the short distance to the fugitives' vehicle.

Drag marks in the gravel beside the empty SUV and drops of blood on the rear bumper sent a deadening chill rippling across the surface of Daisy's skin. For a few seconds she stayed crouched beside the SUV, paralyzed with dread at the thought of what the cops might ultimately find inside the building when they arrived. Maybe it was already too late to save her mom.

She forced her focus back to the task at hand and unfolded the knife. She pressed the tip of the blade into the sidewall of the passenger rear tire of the fugitives' SUV, keeping the vehicle between herself and the building in case either of the bad guys happened to step outside. The air escaped from the tire and the SUV tilted downward.

Determined to learn everything she could to help the cops when they arrived, Daisy moved to the back of the SUV where she could get a quick look at the recreation hall while still remaining mostly hidden. From her position she couldn't see the main entrance of the building, which faced Lake Dillon, but she could see windows on her side of the building. They were boarded over for the season. She also saw a couple of wooden planks that must have been put in place to secure the exit door from the kitchen but were now lying on the ground. They'd obviously been pried off and tossed aside.

Now it seemed very likely that the bad guys were in there.

Daisy desperately wanted to spring into action, rush into the building and rescue her mother. But given the situation, she knew the smartest thing to do was to wait. She was determined to do that. Until she heard Shannon scream, *"No!"*

Instinct kicked in and Daisy found herself racing for the kitchen door with her gun drawn. She stopped short and then slowly pulled it open, standing behind it to give herself a little bit of protection in case someone was waiting to take a shot at her. Of course, a bullet could still blast through the door. When nothing happened, she moved around to peer inside.

Her gaze fell on the empty commercial kitchen. She saw remnants set aside on the countertop where someone had heated up part of a gallon-sized can of clam chowder. Illumination spilling over from lights turned on in the dining hall, which was not in direct view from the kitchen, allowed Daisy to see smeared blood on the floor. The winters in Montana were harsh, so it was common for electricity to be left on even when a building was not being used during cold weather so that minimal heating could keep the pipes from freezing.

But whoever prepped the building for the winter would not have left the lights on.

Daisy crossed over the threshold into the kitchen, took a couple more steps and then stopped.

"Let me go!" Shannon demanded loudly, her voice echoing in the dining hall just around the corner. The gag over her mouth that Daisy had seen in the video must have worked its way free. That was not a surprise. Shannon Lopez was a fighter. Despite her fear for her mother, Daisy felt a faint, hopeful smile cross her lips.

Then she heard something. Like the squeak of a floorboard being stepped on. It came from the dining hall. The kitchen floor was linoleum, but the rest of the flooring in the building was wood plank. Maybe Daltrey or Bunker had seen Daisy when she'd first opened the kitchen door. Maybe one of them was waiting for her to move farther inside until they could get a clear shot at her.

Daisy reached for her phone and considered taking a quick glance at the screen. Maybe Alvis had sent her a text letting her know how soon the cops would arrive. Maybe they were already here. But looking away from her surroundings, even for a second, could be a fatal mistake.

The sound of wood splintering and a whoosh of cool air snapped her attention back to the dining hall, tempting her to quickly move around the corner so she could see what was happening. But she needed to stay as calm as possible. She needed to be smart. She could tell that sunlight was spilling into the building from the direction of the dining hall. And she could hear scuffling noises, like the sound of a struggle. She heard her mother's voice again, only this time it was muffled.

A car engine started up. The sound didn't come from the direction of the SUV with the now-deflated tire, but from the other side of the building. From the dining hall. What was going on? Did they have a second vehicle?

The sound of three rapid gunshots had Daisy sprinting around the corner and into the dining hall, ready to do whatever was necessary to protect her mother. The first thing that caught her attention was a side door hanging open with bright sunlight streaming in. She saw Daltrey, tall and slender with ice-blue eyes, standing by the doorway. Bunker was nowhere in sight. Daltrey pointed a gun at her. She ducked out of the way as three more shots rang out, the bullets tearing up the wood paneling behind the spot where she'd just been standing.

The instant the gunfire stopped, Daisy peeked around the corner into the dining hall again. The side door hung open, and she could see a pickup truck pulling away. There was a motionless body lying in a corner.

They'd killed her mom.

Dear Lord. Sick with fear, Daisy rushed over to the body and dropped to her knees.

It *wasn't* her mom. It was Jimmy Nestor, a roughly forty-year-old small-time criminal whom Daisy had run across many times during her bounty hunting career. He was known for his willingness to do anything for money. He must have helped Daltrey and Bunker, told them this rec center would be a good place for a hideout. And this was how they'd paid him for his assistance. One or both of them had shot him in the chest multiple times. Daisy checked for a pulse despite the man's catastrophic injuries. He was gone.

Daisy sat back on her heels, needing a few seconds to steady her nerves and recover from the wallop of fear and shock she'd felt when she'd thought her mother had been murdered.

After a couple of deep breaths, she got to her feet, hurried over to the open side door and stepped outside. The truck was nowhere in sight, but the paved road out here ended with a loop around the lake, so the fugitives would be forced to go back out the way they came in. She turned and jogged toward Alvis, who was already rushing in her direction yelling, "What happened?"

Daisy had barely uttered a few words of explanation when she saw a flicker of red and blue lights through the pine forest in the direction of the road. The reality of her situation hit her all at once. The criminals she was chasing weren't stupid. *She* was. They'd set a trap and she'd walked right into it. They'd wanted her to find them. And then leaving her on the scene with a dead body meant she'd be tied up for the rest of the day being interviewed by the cops while Daltrey and Bunker made their getaway. The added benefit for the bad guys would be that local police resources would be stretched thin as the cops now had to investigate the murder of Jimmy Nestor along with the kidnapping of Shannon Lopez.

She started hurrying toward her SUV, Alvis right behind her, while mentally beating herself up for being so foolish. She realized now that she might be in over her head pursuing two professional killers who were this calculating. But she wasn't going to let that stop her from doing everything she could.

"When the cops get here, tell them I couldn't stay," she said to Alvis as she pulled her key fob out of her pocket. "But I'll come into the police department to give a statement later."

Alvis shook his head. "That's not how it works. You need to stay here."

"I've got to go." Daisy slid behind the wheel of her SUV. She needed to leave before the police rolled up and detained her.

"What exactly do you think you're going to do?" Alvis snapped.

"I'm going to keep hunting them." She connected her phone with her vehicle's hands-free device. "First, I'm going to call them and see if they respond. Then I'm going to do anything and everything I can think of. I've *got* to find them before they hurt my mom."

She hit the gas and drove away.

Martin Silverdeer barreled toward Jameson driving a bit over the speed limit. The thing that kept him from flooring his truck's gas pedal was the realization that he could get pulled over and then it would take him even longer to get to Daisy.

He *had* to get to Daisy and make sure she was okay. He was desperate to make certain Shannon Lopez was safe, as well. Mrs. Lopez was like a second mother to him.

Shortly before Martin's senior year of high school, when his parents were going through yet another round in a series of ceaseless—and sometimes violent— clashes, Martin's great-aunt Rachel and great-uncle Oliver had suggested he get out of Stone River, Idaho, for a while and come stay with them in Jameson, Montana.

He'd jumped at the chance, and had quickly made friends at school with Aaron Lopez, who brought him home to meet his family, including his kid sister, Daisy.

Now, ten years later, Martin couldn't possibly put into words what he felt for Daisy. It was a combination of so many different emotions. It was also the one single reality of Daisy being *Daisy*. She was quick-witted and funny, brave and determined, understanding and compassionate.

Their relationship was complicated. She was his best friend's little sister. Plus, he and Daisy had a history of friendship and he was afraid of messing that up if he acted on the romantic feelings he couldn't help having for her.

Aaron Lopez had joined the military right out of high school. He was a career United States marine who spent a lot of time serving overseas. The night before Aaron initially left Jameson to report for basic training, he'd asked Martin to look after his mom and sister while he was away. Not that he thought they were incompetent. Far from it. They were both strong women. But Aaron was aware that the world was a dangerous place. And that people needed to look out for one another.

Ten years later, Martin still took that request seriously. And when he'd gotten the call from Daisy's boss, Alvis, telling him about the kidnapping and what had just happened at the rec center, Martin had felt his heart nearly drop to the floor. He'd told his own boss at Rock Solid Bail Bonds, Cassie Wheeler, that he had to leave the office immediately and why. She'd waved him out the door and told him to let her know if he needed any help.

Martin was nearly at the end of the two-hour drive from Stone River to Jameson when his phone rang. It was Cassie. "The cops are searching for Daisy right now for questioning," she said as soon as Martin answered. "I've gotten calls from the Jameson PD and the Beckett County Sheriff's Department asking if I know anything that could help them find her."

"Yeah, well, I don't have any information for you to pass along to them," Martin said. And even if he did have information, he would keep it to himself. At least until he talked to Daisy. This was a dangerous situation on many levels right now. He was afraid some overexcited cop might put Daisy in harm's way in their haste to find her and take her into custody. Because if he knew Daisy, she wouldn't make it easy for them to stop her from doing her best to rescue her mom.

"Martin, I know how much you care about Daisy," Cassie said. "It's obvious by the look on your face and the tone of your voice anytime you talk about her. But I'm warning you to be careful. You don't know what you're walking into." She sighed. "People change. Even people you know. Or *think* you know. They'll do things that will surprise you."

He understood what Cassie was implying. That maybe Daisy wasn't the upright, trustworthy person he thought she was. But he knew better than that. In fact, he believed in her enough that if he'd handled things better, if he'd been able to shake off the fear that he might turn out to be like his parents, he would have proposed to her a long time ago.

There'd been a few weeks a couple of years ago when Daisy had flirted with him, but instead of flirting back, he'd frozen up in fear. And the same fear still haunted him.

What if he was like his parents? He didn't lose his temper and get violent like they did. He never would. That was a commitment he'd made to himself in his early teens, and he'd stuck to it. But fear triggered by the realization that he didn't actually know how to make a relationship work had sunk its roots deeply into him. Kept him from taking a chance at letting their relationship turn into something more than friendship.

He couldn't stand the thought of being a disappointment to Daisy. Or ruining things between them. But he could love her from a distance. And hide his feelings. Although he apparently hadn't done a very good job of hiding them from Cassie.

"I've tried to call Daisy multiple times," Martin said. "She won't answer. I'm in touch with Alvis. He's been trying to talk to her and she isn't answering his calls, either. He says thanks to people overhearing the police radio traffic about the person shot and killed at the rec hall, and then gossiping about it on social media, rumors are flying around that Daisy was actually the shooter. Some fool started speculating that she's turned into a vigilante in order to rescue her mom."

"I'm sorry to hear that," Cassie said.

Martin sighed heavily. "The police have posted statements on their own social media accounts trying to squash the rumors. Maybe it will help eventually. But right now she needs my help, whether she knows it or not. I'll call you when I have an update."

He disconnected and called Daisy's number. It went to voice mail, just like it had all the other times. Once again, he left a message, making it clear he knew what was going on, only this time he didn't hide his frustration. "I'm almost to Jameson," he snapped. "I haven't called your brother yet to tell him what's going on, but if I have to, I will. I'm here to help you. Whatever it takes. Call me back. Now." He was banking on her tendency to withhold bad news from Aaron. In her brother's line of work, being distracted could get him killed.

A minute after he disconnected, his phone rang. It was Daisy.

"Tell me where you are," he said when he answered, too scared for her safety to bother with a polite greeting.

After a few seconds of silence on her end, he tried again. This time he spoke a little more calmly. "It's just me," he said. "No one else is listening in. I'm not trying to corner you. I need to see you. I need to understand what's going on."

"They've got Mom," she said, sounding both defiant and fragile at the same time.

The sharp pain in his heart at the sound of her voice made it hard for him to breathe. "We'll get her back." He forced himself to sound calm. "You and me. Together. Tell me where you are."

"I'm at the Acorn Valley Mall," she said. "Daltrey and Bunker, the bail jumpers from Miami who have Mom, should be here in just a few minutes. I called them and told them I'd trade myself for my mom's freedom."

Martin felt the blood drain from his face. "You can't do that."

"Of course I won't *actually* do it," Daisy responded, with the exaggerated patience she often used when she was mildly annoyed with him. "But I can pretend I will. Alvis always says, 'Work with what you've got.' That's sound advice. And right now, what I've got is that Daltrey and Bunker think I'm stupid.

"I realize now they wanted me to find them up by Lake Dillon. They included the recreation hall in the video they sent me so I'd know where they were. They knew I'd be too afraid for my mom's safety to call the cops. And they knew that if they could get me there, with a dead body on the scene, I'd be so tangled up dealing with the cops that they could get away. They took a chance, and it paid off for them. They know there are rules bounty hunters have to play by if they want to stay on the good side of law enforcement and remain in business. Like reporting dead bodies as soon as they find one. And remaining on the scene."

Martin was already in the middle of the town of Jameson. He turned into the mall parking lot. "You're on the bad side of the cops right now, Daisy. We're going to have to get that straightened out. But, first things first. Where exactly are you?"

"Behind the movie theater." The theater was in a

separate building on the edge of the mall complex. "Park your rig close to the stores and then walk over here on foot. You can hunker down out of sight in the back seat of my SUV, and hopefully the bad guys won't know that you're here. I haven't seen them, so I don't think they've arrived yet."

"Copy that. Be right there." He parked, then grabbed the bottled water and protein bars he normally kept in his truck.

Much as he wanted to run to her, Martin made himself walk over to the movie theater so as not to draw attention to himself. He could see Daisy watching his approach through her front windshield.

"Hey," he said after opening the door, glancing around to make certain no one was watching, and then climbing in. He quickly lay down on the back seat. "You all right? You injured?"

"I'm worried about Mom," Daisy said dully, sounding as if she was in shock. He couldn't blame her.

"We'll get her back. Here, I brought you something." He passed a bottle of water and a protein bar to her. She tossed the bar onto the passenger seat beside her, but she uncapped the water and took several long swigs.

"So, what's the plan?" Martin asked.

"A straight exchange. They drive up. They both hold on to Mom as they let her out of their vehicle and walk toward me. I walk toward them. They let go of Mom and grab hold of me. That's it." She took a sip of water. "I didn't have time for a fancy plan. I've got a gun. I've got my martial-arts training. I figured I'll come up with some genius move on the fly."

Ah, the Daisy Lopez bravado. Sometimes it got her out of jams. Sometimes it made things worse.

"Well, now that you've got me here to help, what's the new plan?" Martin asked.

"Once my mom's in the clear and they're holding on to me instead of her, we take them down. You pop out of the SUV. They'll be surprised. I pull out my gun and take on whoever is on my right. You take the other one."

A highly risky plan, but they were backed into a corner right now with few options.

Daisy's phone chimed. "No," she muttered. And then much more forcefully she said, "No, no, *no.*"

Martin's gut clenched. Something was obviously wrong. "What's happening?"

"I got a text from the thugs we're chasing. They want to do the exchange in a different location."

Martin's heart sank. A last-minute change made the situation more unpredictable. And much more dangerous.

TWO

"Maybe they saw me when I walked over here," Martin said from the back seat, where he was still trying to stay out of sight. "Maybe that's why they're changing the exchange location."

Daisy took a quick look at her surroundings while fighting a sensation of deflating hope that she'd ever see her mother alive again.

She'd already lost her father to a hit-and-run driver when she was seventeen. Determined that the unknown offender would be brought to justice after the official police investigation had grown cold, she'd made it a point to visit every auto body repair shop in the county on a regular basis in the months following the accident to remind the mechanics to stay on the lookout for a vehicle with a distinctive front grille. She brought along photos of her dad's damaged pickup truck showing the imprint from the grille so the mechanics would have a clear idea of what to look for.

A little over a year after the fatal accident, thanks to an employee at an auto body shop who tipped off the police, the hit-and-run driver was caught. And Daisy re-

alized what she wanted to do for a living. She wanted to
track down people who thought they were above the law.
She believed in forgiveness. But she also believed that
people needed to take responsibility for their actions.

Like now. Beau Daltrey and Ivan Bunker needed
to face their murder charges out of Miami, plus new
charges of kidnapping her mom and murdering Jimmy
Nestor.

At the Acorn Valley Mall, Daisy had parked with
the theater building on her right and a vacant lot dot-
ted with clusters of trees on her left. There were no vehicles directly in front of her SUV or behind it. There
were no movie patrons milling around since it was a
weekday, and there were no scheduled movie showings
until later this evening.

"I don't see anyone watching us," she said to Martin.
"And if they did see you arrive, it's too late to hide that
fact now. You might as well sit up front with me."

In an instant, he was in the seat beside her. Martin
often moved like that, fast and light on his feet. Daisy's
early bounty hunting experiences had gotten him interested in the profession and he'd turned out to be a
natural at it. Cassie Wheeler had hired him and helped
him hone his skills. On the occasions when Daisy had
bounty hunted with him, she'd seen him outrun every
fugitive who'd tried to flee from him. Often, he approached his target so stealthily that the person never
saw him coming.

Martin reached across from the passenger seat and
lightly squeezed her upper arm. "We *will* rescue your
mom," he said, looking at her with dark brown eyes
filled with strength and compassion.

Daisy nodded, and then quickly turned away as tears began to sting her eyes. Seeing Martin again released a painful feeling of reassurance. Like the burning sensation when warmth returned to a nearly frozen extremity. Having him here tempted her to let go for a moment and surrender the fight to hold back her fear and terror over possibly losing her mom. Martin would have her back. She could trust him absolutely. Especially when facing a life-or-death situation. Like now.

But this was not the time to give in to her feelings. Especially when those stubborn emotions, unchecked, tended toward something beyond friendship. Martin was not a settling-down kind of guy. As long as she'd known him, he'd never been involved in a serious romantic relationship. She knew he dated, but he'd never talked to her about wanting a serious relationship with a woman. Any woman. And there was no reason to think that would change.

She turned to him. "Thank you for coming." She patted his hand where it gripped her arm and he dropped it back to his lap. "I'm texting them a reply." She typed out "What now?" and sent it.

"This whole situation is so odd," Martin said.

Daisy watched him look around, appearing to momentarily focus on the clusters of trees, the only places where anyone could possibly hide and not be in plain sight. "Why didn't Daltrey and Bunker just get out of Jameson? Or hunker down and stay out of sight for a while? Why all the drama?"

"I've been thinking about that." Daisy stared at her phone, anxiously waiting for a reply to her text. She'd gotten a lot of texts and phone calls from people over the last couple of hours but she'd ignored them. Things had started spiraling out of control when she first got the video of her mom, and they just kept spiraling. She had no idea how she was going to straighten things out with law enforcement. She'd deal with all of that later. Rescuing her mom was where she needed to focus her thoughts right now.

"The obvious conclusion is that we're not dealing with our normal, run-of-the-mill bounty who's running in a blind panic." Daisy looked up at Martin. "Daltrey and Bunker have a strategy, and the foundation of that strategy is confusion. That's what I think. They want to keep me and the cops off balance until they can make a clean getaway.

"They had been hunkering down in Jameson for about five weeks when I came across enough evidence to convince me that they were here, and I started hunting them in earnest. I almost had them. They know that if they stay, I *will* capture them." She nodded at Martin. "Or some other bounty hunter will. Or maybe the cops. I imagine they realize by now that it would have been smarter for them to try to hide in a big city.

"I think they're willing to exchange my mom for me because it gets them a hostage for leverage if they end up having to negotiate with the cops, *and* it means they have one less determined bounty hunter tracking them. If they try to drive out of town right now, there's an excellent chance the Montana Highway Patrol will intercept them. Even if they steal a different vehicle, they'll still have to stop and get gas for it. And by now their pictures are posted at gas stations all over the region," she continued.

"My guess is that they want to get everyone running in circles, and then maybe they'll make a break for it. Or maybe this is all meant to buy them enough time for their organized crime cronies to show up and help them out."

There were so many possibilities.

Most of Daisy's bounties weren't exactly geniuses. They'd stay out of sight for a few days, maybe a couple of weeks, and then they'd fall back to their old habits. They'd go back to visit their friends or family, or return to their favorite restaurant or bar, and Daisy would nab them.

Sometimes her targets were connected to more sophisticated drug distribution rings. Particularly the ones who lurked around the university. Oftentimes those bail jumpers had the smarts and the means to spirit themselves out of town, and they ended up on some other bounty hunter's capture list in their new destination.

A few fugitives, typically from other regions of the country, seemed to think they could hide out in the wilderness until people gave up looking for them. As if Daisy or any other Montana-based bounty hunter couldn't follow them into the surrounding mountains or forest. Those were the hunts where Martin's expertise came in especially handy, and he'd pop over to Jameson, with perhaps another hunter from Rock Solid Bail Bonds in nearby Idaho, to help her out.

In the end, with the wilderness hiders, if they weren't a serious threat to public safety, it was often better to just play the long game and wait them out. Winter was a real force in Montana. And when people got hungry and cold enough, they came back into town.

Daltrey and Bunker, compared with her past targets, were a pair of wild cards. Completely out of the ordinary. Smart, with a unique strategy. They were dangerous fugitives who'd kidnapped her mom. Daisy's worst nightmare had come true. Her job had put a member of her family in danger. And right now, she was absolutely stumped about what to do next.

"Dear Lord, please guide, strengthen and protect us," she prayed softly, while continuing to scan the area around them, keeping her eyes open while she prayed in case Daltrey and Bunker had somehow escaped detection and were about to launch a surprise attack. "Please protect my mom. And help her to remember that You're there with her, even if it doesn't feel like it. Amen."

"Amen," Martin affirmed.

Daisy's phone chimed. The thugs had sent another video. This one showed Shannon, looking ashen and staring toward the camera. This time she didn't have a gag in her mouth and she didn't look like she was tied up. The focus widened to show that her mom was seated at a table in a public place, with people walking behind her. Ivan Bunker sat very close to her. The shorter of the two fugitives had his right arm around her shoulder and his left hand below the tabletop and out of sight. Probably pressing a gun against Shannon's side. His reddish hair had grown out since his official booking photo had been taken and he wore a smirk on his face.

Daisy had seen those white, metal, bistro-style tables before. Two neon signs shone behind them, one advertising pizza and the other offering Chinese food. "They're at the food court inside the mall," she said.

The video abruptly ended, and by that time a text

from the criminals had arrived. Enter through the north entrance at the food court. Hands held away from your body so we can see them. You have five minutes.

"Makes sense they'd want to do the exchange there," Martin responded. "Lots of innocent people around, including children. Daltrey and Bunker know we won't shoot or do anything to risk hurting the civilians. Meanwhile, they won't feel the slightest bit constrained. They won't think twice about putting people in danger."

While Martin talked, Daisy drove toward the north side of the mall.

"Let me go in first," Martin said as Daisy parked the SUV. "Give me a minute to get into place. I'll head for one of the food counters close to them. After the exchange, when your mom is in the clear and they're taking you out the door, I'll come up from behind and we'll jump them."

They hurried toward the mall, stopping just out of sight of anyone who might be inside looking through the glass doors. After taking a deep breath, Martin slowly resumed walking toward the entrance, glancing around as though he didn't have a care in the world.

Daisy's heart thundered in her chest. It wasn't only her mother who was in danger now. Martin was, too. Once he made his move, anything could happen.

The three minutes she waited outside, where she remained out of view from the inside of the mall and couldn't see what was happening, felt like the longest three minutes of her life. The familiar shot of adrenaline in anticipation of a capture coursed through her body, making her hands tremble slightly. She wanted to rush in, rescue her mother and bust the two fugitives *right now*. But she'd agreed to let Martin have time to get into place. And she'd disciplined herself to be patient early in her bounty hunting career when she saw how often that paid off. Still, she had to keep checking the time on her phone to make sure she didn't jump the gun.

Finally, she took a deep breath and then headed for the door. Her hand was steady now as she reached for the handle. Once inside, she immediately spotted her mom. Ivan Bunker was still seated with his arm around Shannon, like he'd been in the video. Beau Daltrey stood beside the table.

She fought the temptation to look around for Martin, aware that such an action might tip off the bad guys that she had someone helping her right there in the food court. Daltrey, a tall, skinny guy with a horseshoe-shaped ring of blond hair atop an otherwise bald head, glared at Daisy. He gestured toward her hands, and she immediately held them away from her body so he could see she wasn't carrying a gun. Not in her hands, anyway. She did have one tucked into the waistband at the small of her back.

She shifted her gaze to her mom, who was looking at her with eyes rapidly filling with tears. Shannon locked gazes with Daisy and then shook her head, mouthing the words, *No, don't do this*.

Shannon did not want her daughter to trade places with her. She must have overheard Daltrey and Bunker as they talked about their plans. And her mom would have recognized Martin when he walked in and guessed what was about to happen.

Daisy knew her mom's heart. Shannon Lopez would not want anyone else to be put in danger for her sake.

But Daisy didn't always follow her mom's directions. Sometimes life forced a person to make a tough choice among options, none of which were ideal. Daisy had faced that dilemma several times since she'd become a bounty hunter. That didn't mean she was comfortable with it, but she did have experience at steeling her resolve and doing what needed to be done.

Daisy continued to move toward them. From the corner of her eye, she caught a glimpse of Martin at the counter of the pizza place just a few steps away. At Daisy's approach, Ivan Bunker, the shorter and stockier of the two hit men, got to his feet, pulling Shannon up with him.

Daisy's muscles tensed as the moment neared when Bunker would set her mother free. Daisy would walk with Bunker and Daltrey outside, pretending to be their new hostage, until Martin came out behind them. At which point the two bounty hunters could make their move and arrest the thugs. And this nightmare would finally be over.

She was nearly within reach, just about to the point when Bunker could let go of her mother and grab hold of Daisy at the same time, when a male voice yelled out, "Daisy! Daisy Lopez! A lot of people are looking for you." It was Kevin Bosanko, a Jameson emergency medical technician whom Daisy had interacted with many times in the course of her work.

Several patrons in the food court turned in her direction. The EMT shifted the trajectory he'd been walking and started heading directly toward her.

Ivan Bunker's eyes widened. He frantically looked around while tightening his grip on Shannon's arm and yanking her closer to him. "Stay away!" He raised the gun he'd been hiding beneath his coat, pointing it toward Kevin. Daltrey also drew a handgun, waving it at the small crowd watching them. He shoved over the bistro table and tossed the chairs toward Kevin, creating a small, temporary barricade. Kevin froze in his tracks. Daltrey and Bunker started backing toward the glass doors, forcing Shannon to go with them.

Daisy looked to her mom, so close, but still out of her reach. "Let her go, and we'll let you go," Daisy called out.

Martin was already on the move, rapidly cutting a diagonal path toward the exit that could put him behind the gunmen where he might be able to get the jump on them. She and Martin were going to have to do something, *now.* The gun at the small of her back felt especially heavy. She was tempted to reach for it, but there were too many innocent people here, many of them very young children. She couldn't risk escalating the situation.

Before Martin could get into place, Bunker caught sight of him and pointed his gun in Martin's direction. He obviously didn't want anyone getting behind him. Martin stopped in his tracks.

The two kidnappers made it out the door with Shannon. Martin was right behind them, with Daisy hot on his heels. A trio of shoppers unwisely followed them outside, two of them yelling into their phones, describing what was happening, while the third appeared to be videotaping everything.

Daltrey and Bunker were nearly to their truck, each of them clutching one of Shannon's arms and forcing her along with them, when Daltrey spun and fired toward the civilians.

"Get down!" Daisy shouted to the shoppers as she and Martin took cover behind a parked car. She heard the truck peeling out of the parking lot, and stood up in time to watch it turn onto the road and disappear from sight.

Martin was already on the phone with 9-1-1, calling in the emergency and giving a description of the truck and its plate number. Daisy listened to his call while a wave of numbness and despair overcame her. She'd had this one chance to save her mother's life, and she'd blown it.

If there were a way Martin could remove the burden of heartache and fear that Daisy was carrying and place it on his own shoulders, he would do it.

Eight hours had passed since the shooting at the shopping mall. Daisy and Martin were now at the Peak Bail Bonds office. The local TV news stations were covering the story of Shannon's kidnapping and the altercation at the shopping mall, including showing mug shots of Daltrey and Bunker. That might ultimately help with the bail jumpers' capture, but in the meantime, there'd been no reported sighting of them or the truck they'd escaped in. And no confirmation that Shannon Lopez was still alive.

Daisy had sent several texts to the criminals and had tried to call them, but they had not responded. The authorities had pinged the phone's location, which sent them to a neighborhood a couple of blocks away from the mall. A search of the area, including door-to-door canvasses of the residents, had turned up nothing. Martin figured the thugs had likely flung the phone out the window while fleeing so that the cops wouldn't be able to find them. It was probably lying undiscovered on the ground some-where in the vicinity, maybe under some bushes, or per-haps it had slid into a storm drain.

"Given the situation, I can't honestly say that I would have done things any differently than you did today," Sheriff Grace Russell said to Daisy.

Martin was standing near Daisy. He'd made a point of staying by her side as the investigation of the day's events dragged out during a seemingly endless after-noon and into the early evening.

"But leaving the scene after finding a dead body is not the right thing to do," the Beckett County sheriff continued. "It's especially egregious for a bounty hunter who is working a case. You have responsibilities that go with your job. You understand that, right?"

"Yes, ma'am," Daisy answered quietly.

The sheriff went on to make eye contact with Martin, Alvis and Millie Carter, pausing to get a verbal affirma-tion from each one of them indicating that they under-stood her directive. She hadn't come down as hard as she could have on Daisy. But she obviously also wanted to make sure everyone knew exactly what her expectations were in a situation that resulted in a fatality.

They were standing in the lobby of the bail bonds office. The business was housed on the bottom floor of a three-story Victorian-style house. The second floor had been partitioned into two studio apartments. Daisy rented one of the apartments. The other one was currently vacant. Owners Alvis Carter and his wife, Millie, lived on the top floor.

Justine DePaul and Steve Reynoso, both of whom worked part-time at skip tracing and general office work, were still seated at desks nearby. The nature of the bail bond business led to office hours that typically started later in the day and ran until evening.

From local law enforcement's point of view, the Daltrey and Bunker crime spree had started with the kidnapping of Shannon Lopez from her home outside the city limits. That put it under the jurisdiction of the Beckett County Sheriff's Department. The Jameson Police Department would be supporting the investigation.

The sheriff was a tall woman with platinum blond hair tied back in a severe bun. She'd worked her way up through the ranks over the years before finally being elected sheriff, and she was known for her straightforward manner.

She turned her sharp gaze on Daisy. "I do realize that you chose your course of action because you were worried about the safety of your mother. I want you to know that we're doing everything we can to find her, including working with multiple law enforcement agencies and using all available resources. Please keep us apprised of everything you are doing to find your mom. And if the kidnappers contact you again, let us know. We need to work together."

"I understand," Daisy said. Which, Martin noted, wasn't exactly an agreement to do what the sheriff had asked. Sheriff Russell tilted her head slightly, and Martin figured she'd picked up on that small detail, as well.

The sheriff strode to the door and stopped. "I probably don't need to say this, but I'll say it anyway. Keep all the doors and windows on this place locked tight. I'm sure you've got some kind of security system. Double-check that it's working properly. Given the stunts our two fugitives have already pulled, there's no telling what they'll do next."

"Yes, ma'am," Alvis said.

The sheriff put on her cream-colored Stetson hat before bidding everyone a good night and walking out the door.

At that point, Millie sent Justine and Steve home and started closing up the office. "It's been a long day, for you most of all," she said to Daisy. She glanced at her husband and then at Martin. "But I'm sure all of us could use some rest. This is a good night to turn in early." She turned her attention to Daisy again. "We'll get back on the hunt first thing tomorrow. And remember, while you're sleeping, law enforcement is out looking for your mom. They're doing everything they can to find her."

Martin gestured toward the leather couch in the small lobby. "I'll sack out here for the night."

"You don't have to stay," Daisy said.

She'd seemed oddly detached in her interactions with people since the shooting at the mall. Even her voice sounded different. Unemotional almost to the point of sounding robotic. Martin figured it was due to shock, or trauma, or fatigue. Or maybe all of the above.

He looked at the lost expression in her eyes and wanted to take her in his arms so badly he could hardly restrain himself. But each time he'd tried to hug her today, or tried to wrap an arm around her shoulder in a side embrace, she'd withdrawn ever so slightly.

Her reaction had stung, but once Martin realized what she was doing, he'd held himself back. She'd been through so much. He could only imagine what she was feeling. If she wanted him to give her some distance, he would do that. He'd back off. But he wouldn't leave her side. He'd sleep in his truck out in the parking lot if he had to.

"The second apartment upstairs is empty. You'll stay there," Millie said matter-of-factly. After one final check of the first-floor locks on the doors and windows, along with the alarm settings, she and Alvis started up the stairs toward their own living quarters at the very top of the building. "I'll bring some bed linens and towels down to the empty apartment for you," Millie called back to him.

With a heavy sigh, Daisy started up the stairs and Martin followed her. At the second-floor hallway, he watched her walk to her apartment door, open it and flick on an overhead light. But then she came back and stood at the threshold, waiting there with Martin until Millie came back down with an armload of linens. Millie insisted on getting things set up for Martin and disappeared into the apartment.

"I can't believe all of this is happening," Daisy said after a couple of minutes of silence.

"Me, neither," Martin said. "But we'll get your mom back. Or the cops will. Everybody's looking, and there are only so many ways to get out of Jameson."

She nodded.

"Right now, the best thing you can do is try to get

a little shut-eye," he added, knowing that she probably wouldn't sleep very well. "Tomorrow, we'll pick up their trail."

Martin had already gotten Millie to forward to him all of the information Peak Bail Bonds had received from the bail bondsman in Florida who'd requested their help to capture Daltrey and Bunker. He planned to spend the night poring over everything and learning all that he could about the two men and their organized crime connections.

Millie came out of the apartment a few minutes later. "Everything's ready for you," she said to Martin. Then she stepped across the narrow hallway to give Daisy a hug followed by a kiss on the cheek. Martin couldn't help noticing that Daisy didn't pull away from her. "Don't you lose hope, honey."

"No, ma'am," Daisy said, her voice barely louder than a whisper. "I won't."

"Good night." Millie went back upstairs.

Daisy looked across the hall at Martin, her face becoming flushed and tears starting to roll down her cheeks. She gave him a quick nod before she stepped back inside her apartment and closed the door.

With a heavy heart, Martin went into his own apartment and shut his door. As time passed, the odds of recovering Shannon Lopez alive faded. While Daisy, hopefully, got some rest, he would open the case files and get to work reviewing them, praying all the while that he would notice some detail that would lead to the fugitives' capture and Shannon's rescue.

THREE

Daisy's eyes felt sore and gritty, but at least she wasn't crying anymore. Not at the moment, anyway.

It was morning, shortly after sunrise. Twenty-one hours since she'd received the video showing her mother being held captive. She'd already checked her phone several times looking for news updates about her mom or any communication from the sheriff's department, but there was nothing new.

Last night had brought a fitful combination of nightmare-riddled sleep and agonized wakefulness drenched with worry. Daisy had prayed. *A lot.* She knew her mom would be praying, too. While weathering an emotional storm that reminded her of how she'd felt after her father was killed, she'd repeatedly reminded herself that the situation now was not the same as it had been back then. Her mother had not been killed. She was *alive*. Daisy was determined to believe that until someone could prove otherwise.

The experience with her father's death had taught her she could lean on her faith *and* take action at the same time. That's what she had to do now. She already had a plan. She was dressed and ready to resume the hunt for the lowlifes who'd kidnapped her mom.

The cops would be covering the roadways and airport in their search, as well as tracking any electronic activity like credit card or cell phone use. Daisy figured the best way for her to start hunting for the fugitives was to go back to the point when she'd first realized they were almost within her grasp. From there, she might be able to develop new leads on where the kidnappers might go or what they might do next.

She'd left a real estate office just moments before finding out that Shannon had been kidnapped. Prior to that, she'd spent days visiting hotels, motels and real estate offices that rented vacation properties. Yesterday morning, Jill at Mountain Lakes Realty had recognized a photo of Beau Daltrey. She said he'd rented a house from her, but he'd used a different name. When Daisy asked for the address of the property and if she could see his rental application, Jill had gotten nervous and said she needed to talk to her boss before giving out that information.

At her request, Daisy and Alvis had waited outside while Jill made the call.

And then the awful texts had started arriving on Daisy's phone and she and Alvis had left.

This morning Daisy wanted to go back to the realty office. She was determined to see what information Daltrey had offered in his rental application. He had no doubt lied for the most part, but maybe he'd accidentally given some truthful piece of information she could use to track down him and his criminal partner.

Once she found the location of the rental house, she

would search it for clues the men might have left behind. She would look around even if the owner refused to give her permission. She'd figure out a way to get inside. If this were a normal situation, she'd do things by the book. But when Daltrey and Bunker grabbed her mother, this stopped being a normal pursuit.

She had told Sheriff Russell everything she knew yesterday, including the lead she'd uncovered on where the hit men had been staying for the last couple of weeks. Thanks to the sheriff, she now knew the exact address of the property. Odds were good that some member of law enforcement had already been out to search the house. A couple of more bounty hunters wandering through it looking for clues the cops might have overlooked shouldn't be that big of a problem at this point.

Determined to get some useful work done today, Daisy snapped her handcuffs and pepper spray onto her belt, slid her gun into her holster and grabbed the daypack that functioned as a purse as well as a storage case for her electronic tablet. She opened her door, quietly stepped out and shut it behind her. She stared at Martin's closed door across the hall, trying to decide what she wanted to do about him.

Having Martin by her side made her feel better in the midst of this horrible situation. A *lot* better. He was smart. He was competent. She could trust him with her life. He had depth, but he was also often the first person in a tense situation to say something to lighten the mood. He was a man of faith.

For all of those reasons, and more, working with Martin triggered some very inconvenient emotions.

Martin had stayed safely tucked in the realm of "my brother's friend" for years. And then things had changed. At least for Daisy. About a year and a half ago, Martin had come to Jameson to visit for a week when Aaron was home on leave. And for some unknown reason, Daisy found herself feeling something toward Martin that was definitely a "more than a friend" vibe.

She'd been caught off guard by it. Stunned. She couldn't keep her eyes off Martin when they were in the same room. And they were in the same room a lot because he was staying at her mom's house. She'd caught herself grinning at him for no particular reason. When he smiled at her in return, her heart had actually fluttered in her chest. It was mortifying.

After the second full day of embarrassing giddiness, she'd begun to wonder, "Why not Martin?" She'd reached a point where she was looking to settle down, get married, raise a family. And she knew Martin was a good man. So, she'd flirted with him a little. Subtly, she'd thought. Instead of welcoming her overtures, he'd seemed terrified. And he'd started putting the maximum amount of space between them every chance he got.

It was insulting. And she'd felt like a fool. But okay, fine. Martin didn't want to be more than friends.

Daisy had been disappointed, but she'd accepted his apparent decision. And so, they'd remained friends. With one small hiccup. Daisy couldn't get rid of that "more than a friend" feeling for him. And she couldn't tell if that was clouding her judgment on the case they were working right now.

Would it be better if she and Martin split up and followed separate leads, looking to uncover more answers faster? Or was it smarter and more reasonable for the two of them to work together as a team?

Martin's door opened. He stood at the threshold, smiling at her, dressed and looking like he was ready to get rolling. "Good morning."

"Good morning," Daisy responded, while an unwelcome flutter of delight tickled the center of her stomach.

He crossed his arms and slowly leaned his lanky frame against the doorway.

Daisy had a moment when she couldn't quite catch her breath.

"I heard your door open and waited for you to knock," he said. "After a while, I thought you might think I was still asleep. I wanted to make sure you didn't go out looking for your mom without me." The smile on his lips faded slightly, and the expression in his eyes turned more solemn. "Wherever you're going today, I'm going with you." He shifted his weight and his smile disappeared. "It must have been a rough night for you. Did you get any sleep at all?"

"I'm fine." She didn't want to talk about how she slept or how her night was. She was sick of wallowing in her feelings. What she wanted to do was get to work finding her mother. She told him about her plan to search Daltrey and Bunker's rental house.

"Sounds like a good idea." He nodded in agreement. "I've read up on Daltrey and Bunker and studied their photos."

"Good."

"And I talked to Cassie a few minutes ago. She said Harry and Leon are willing to come over and help."

"Thank you." Harry Orlansky and Leon Bragg were

excellent bounty hunters who worked with Martin at Rock Solid Bail Bonds. "Hopefully we'll have some leads for them to chase down very soon."

The sound of footsteps coming down the stairs from the third floor caught Daisy's attention and she turned to see Millie, who stopped when she was halfway down the staircase.

"You two come up and have breakfast with Alvis and me before you go anywhere."

Daisy shook her head. "Thank you, but we don't have time." She was already feeling guilty for taking time to sleep while her mother was in danger.

"I thought you'd say that. I'm making breakfast burritos. We'll roll one up and you can take it with you." Millie crossed her arms and shot Daisy a defiant look. "You've got to eat something so you'll have enough energy to take care of business today."

"She makes a good point," Martin said. "When's the last time you had a meal? Breakfast, yesterday? Let's eat something. We can make it quick."

"All right."

They followed Millie up the stairs.

The moment Daisy stepped inside the apartment and got a good whiff of the scent of freshly cooked scrambled eggs mixed with green chilies and cheddar cheese, her stomach growled loudly. Martin had been right. It had been twenty-four hours since she'd last eaten. Worry and fear for her mom had deadened her appetite. But now her body demanded that she take care of it. She glanced toward the kitchen and saw Alvis pouring coffee into two thermal mugs sitting on the counter. Back in the living room, the Carters' big fluffy tabby cat, Reggie, sat perched on the top shelf of a bookcase, the tip of his tail twitching. At the bottom of the bookcase, a homely, big-eared, one-eyed pup who looked remarkably like a baby Yoda yipped excitedly.

Alvis had recently come across the puppy, Bowie, at the county dump, where the little dog had been abandoned. Bowie was in love with Reggie. Most of the time, Reggie stoically tolerated the puppy. When he'd had enough adoration, he climbed up out of reach. Millie hushed the dog, and after a couple of more yips, Bowie was finally quiet. But his gaze remained locked on the cat.

"We might as well sit down to eat," Martin suggested to Daisy. "It won't add that much more time."

"And it'll give me a chance to update you on who's helping with the search for your mom and those two losers from Miami while you eat," Alvis said, bringing over the mugs of coffee. "I know I can't physically keep up with a demanding chase anymore, but I can still help out in other ways."

Millie carried over a plate with an egg-filled burrito each for Daisy and Martin. Salsa was already on the table. Alvis and Millie sat down to resume eating the burritos they must have set aside when Millie had gone to invite Daisy and Martin for breakfast.

Daisy spooned salsa over her burrito and dug in. After a few bites, she began to feel stronger.

Alvis explained that he had reached out to all of his and Millie's bounty hunting connections last night in one big email blast, asking for help in the search for and safe return of Shannon Lopez, making it clear that right now the capture of Daltrey and Bunker was a secondary goal. They couldn't afford to ignore the possibility that Shannon and the bad guys had somehow snuck past the cops and gotten out of town. They could be anywhere. So, contacting people across the country to ask for help made sense.

As Daisy and Martin finished their breakfast, Alvis recounted whom he'd heard from and passed along their offers of prayers and help. Several of the respondents expressed their outrage, believing that the kidnapping of one bounty hunter's mother in an attempt to force her to end her pursuit of a target was an attack against all bounty hunters. And that made it personal for them.

After Daisy was done eating, she stood and expressed her thanks to Alvis and Millie for everything they'd done to help her and her mom. The couple brushed aside her expression of appreciation as completely unnecessary.

Millie refilled the travel coffee mugs and set them on the table ready for Daisy and Martin to grab on their way out. Martin cleared his and Daisy's dirty dishes from the table.

Feeling revitalized, Daisy picked up her coffee mug and headed for the door with Martin close behind her. Bowie seemed to think he was going, too, and got underfoot. After nearly stepping on him, Martin reached down to swoop the pup out of the way and handed him over to Millie.

Alvis caught Daisy's gaze just before she walked out the door. "Together, we're going to find your mom. I know we will. Everything will be okay."

"Thank you." Daisy wished she could feel as certain as Alvis sounded. While she and Martin clattered down the two flights of stairs to the bottom floor, she couldn't help thinking about the times when pursuits had gone wrong during her years of bounty hunting. Hunts for the bad guys did not always turn out well. Some people were never found. That was a sad fact. She thought of her mom and choked back the tears, reminding herself to stay focused on the task at hand. Right now, she needed to find some kind of clue to let her know where to look next for her mom and the kidnappers.

"I'm sorry, but I don't have any information that can help you," Louis Stringer, owner of the QuickStop convenience store, said to Daisy. His tone was curt, and he immediately turned away from her.

Martin watched him as he returned to sweeping the floor in front of the popcorn machine. The heavyset man moved stiffly and looked tense. Part of successful bounty hunting included paying attention to body language, and Martin could tell that something was definitely wrong here.

He turned his gaze to Daisy, taking in the expression of surprised disappointment etched on her face. She shook her head. "I don't understand what's happening."

Martin knew that Louis had been willing to help Daisy when she needed information—for a price—since the early days of her bounty hunting career. He'd been at this location in the older part of town for years and he had a pretty good idea of what went on in the neighborhood. But just now, after Daisy had shown him pictures of Beau Daltrey and Ivan Bunker and asked if he'd seen them in this part of town, he'd refused to help her.

Wasn't even willing to *pretend* to help her. Not for twice the money she normally offered him.

Louis had continued sweeping and was now several feet away. Maybe he was out of earshot. Maybe not. "I don't have time for whatever game he's playing," Daisy snapped. "My mother is in danger. I'm going to go find out what his problem is."

"Wait." Martin lightly rested his hand on her shoulder. She glared at him and he dropped his hand. And then he gestured toward the exit. When she stayed stubbornly in place, he walked out the door ahead of her, hoping she'd follow. And she did.

"What?" Daisy demanded after the door closed behind them and they were standing in the parking lot.

Martin took a breath. He understood her impatience. His heart ached when he thought about the fear and pressure she was dealing with. But giving in to that impatience right now was not going to get her what she wanted. "Leaning on Louis too hard might make things worse. You've got a good working relationship with him and you don't want to ruin that. Maybe he's worried that someone will see him talking with you. Daltrey and Bunker are stone-cold killers. Louis has a right to be afraid. Let's walk away for now. You can call him later. Maybe he'll feel safer talking freely over the phone."

Daisy blew out a puff of air. Her face was reddening with anger and frustration. "Something is obviously going on in this part of town and I want to know what it is." She gestured at a beauty salon down the street. "Having Louis refuse to help us like that right after Janis practically ran us out of her hair salon when we tried to show her the photos of Daltrey and Bunker has got me unnerved."

Daisy and Martin had come to this part of town asking questions based on what they'd discovered during their search at the fugitives' rental house.

Jill at the realty office, appearing pale and apologizing profusely for whatever help she'd unintentionally given the thugs, had handed over a key to the property without argument when Daisy and Martin had shown up as soon as they opened. The rental house, a chalet-style structure on the western edge of town with a view of the dramatic Spruce River Gorge, hadn't been a marked crime scene. The cops had already been there and removed the items they'd wanted to inspect more closely, so Daisy and Martin had been able to poke around at will.

There wasn't much of interest inside the house. But the trash was still in the containers outside. Daisy and Martin had dug through it, looking for possible receipts, printed maps, notes that had been jotted down, anything that might tell them something useful. At first, their efforts hadn't looked promising. But then, near the bottom of the heavy green container, Daisy had found a small pizza box from Rizzoli's and a plastic bag from Your Family Store. "These businesses are nowhere near here," Daisy had said. "They're both on the east side of town. Let's go visit them and see if they can tell us anything."

Rizzoli's wasn't open for business early in the morning, but people were inside getting things ready for the day. The employees who let them in were friendly, but they hadn't been able to offer any help and they didn't recognize the mug shots Daisy showed them. The small box she had found in the trash can was used to hold pizza when it was sold by the slice, she was told, so there wouldn't have been an order for it. That was a disappointment since she and Martin had hoped to find a useful clue—like maybe a phone or credit card number—that could help them in their hunt.

One interesting thing that Martin noted while they were there was that the small pizzeria had a pay phone. That was unusual. And that might have been why Daltrey or Bunker would have come here. They could make or take calls on a phone that could not be connected to them personally. Maybe they stayed in contact with their Miami mob bosses that way.

The manager of the restaurant was willing to provide what limited video footage they had only to law enforcement, not to bounty hunters. Daisy texted a summary of what they'd learned to the sheriff. It was not exactly a hot tip that would get a deputy roaring to the restaurant in a patrol car, but maybe the information would eventually turn out to be useful.

After that, they'd gone to Your Family Store, a small shop with a little bit of everything from fishing gear to knitting supplies to inexpensive children's toys. It was an older, run-down building that appeared to stay in business by catering to people who wanted to shop locally or maybe didn't want to make the trip to the big box stores in the newer part of town. Nobody inside the store recognized the photos Daisy showed them. The manager there also was not willing to show the store's security surveillance video to bounty hunters.

Before they left, they'd walked around the store and

Daisy had spotted prepaid phones for sale. "That's it," she said. "Daltrey and Bunker came to this part of town to take care of their need to communicate with their organized crime pals back in Florida. They bought their burner phones here. Maybe they used the pay phone at Rizzoli's when they ran out of minutes on their prepaid phones, or when the weather was terrible and they couldn't get decent reception on the cell phones."

Her theory had made sense to Martin. Like the pizza place, security in the store was very basic. If Daltrey and Bunker bought their phones in a box store or even a gas station, a clear image of them would have been captured on video. In Your Family Store, that would not necessarily have been the case. If they'd paid in cash and refrained from looking up at any of the four high-mounted video cameras Martin had seen inside the store, they would have been able to make their purchase almost invisibly.

Daisy texted that information to the sheriff, as well. A few minutes later she'd received a response thanking her for the information and letting Daisy know that the sheriff's department, Jameson PD and Montana Highway Patrol were all looking hard for her mom and following up on several tips and possible sightings that had been reported.

Convinced that Daltrey and Bunker came to this part of town regularly, Daisy had turned to her informants at the hair salon and the QuickStop convenience store. Now the second of those informants had made it clear he didn't want to get involved.

"Maybe Louis and Janis aren't helping you because they're scared of Daltrey and Bunker's organized crime connections," Martin said while they stood in the parking lot of QuickStop. "The local news stories about them keep emphasizing it."

Daisy nodded. "Maybe so."

With no other leads to pursue at the moment, they decided to visit every business in the area, showing the owners and employees pictures of Daltrey and Bunker, and hoping that someone could confirm that the men spent time in this part of town. If so, then this might be a place where they felt comfortable and would be likely to hide out while the cops were hunting for them. Maybe they would have made friends—perhaps people who didn't realize they were criminals on the run—who were helping them now.

They spent a couple of hours doing that, but it didn't gain them any leads. A few people had seen the mug shots of Daltrey and Bunker on the news, but none claimed to have seen them in person.

Daisy was obviously becoming increasingly worried about her mother. A couple of times when Martin glanced over at her, he saw her wiping tears from her eyes. Empathy for her, and for how Mrs. Lopez must be feeling right now, wrenched his heart.

"Let's take a break," he said to Daisy as they walked down the sidewalk. It was midday, and if they were going to be hunting into the evening, they needed to keep up their strength and energy. He nodded toward a diner up ahead.

"All right," she responded. "But we need to make it quick."

They sat at a booth in the back of the restaurant. Initially, Daisy just asked for coffee. But Martin convinced her to choose something to eat, too, so she added a short stack of pancakes to her order. He was happy to see that she ate half of them. It was better than nothing. He got a meat loaf sandwich and iced tea.

When they were finished eating, Daisy checked in with Alvis. Martin texted Cassie to let her know they didn't need any help from the other Rock Solid Bail Bonds bounty hunters, yet. Then they both scrolled through their phones looking for news updates on the search for Daisy's mom. There wasn't anything significant mentioned on the various news sites they visited, but Martin knew law enforcement agencies often kept information to themselves during active investigations.

"Do you have any ideas on what we should do next?" Daisy asked.

"Let's go down to the sheriff's department." Martin figured they might be able to get some updated information if they went there in person. If nothing else, Daisy would see the people at work trying to find Shannon and that might make her feel a little bit better. It would certainly make *him* feel better. He didn't voice his concerns because he didn't want to add to Daisy's burdens, but it had now been twenty-eight hours since Shannon was kidnapped. And experience had taught him the more time that passed, the less likely they were to recover Mrs. Lopez alive.

Martin paid their bill and they slid out of the booth. Daisy excused herself to visit the ladies' room while Martin headed for the door. It was a sunny day in October, with a bright blue sky overhead and not a cloud in the sky. The temperature was comfortable, but soon enough, winter would make its way here and Jameson would be blanketed with snow.

Martin looked up at the surrounding mountain peaks. He could see a few patches of fall color, but most of what he saw was evergreen. He glanced up and down the street. Thought about Daltrey and Bunker, and how they might try to escape town.

Eventually, after it seemed like a lot of time had passed, he sent Daisy a text. Everything OK?

When he didn't get an immediate response, fear began a cold, icy climb up his spine. He hurried back inside the diner, looking around while calling out her name. He knocked on the door of the ladies' room, and when there was no response, he had a female employee take a look. The employee came out and told him it was empty, so he went in and confirmed it for himself.

Fear clawed at his throat as he ran out the back door into the alley, didn't see Daisy and then hurried back inside and fast-walked through the diner to the front of the building in case they'd just missed each other. She wasn't there.

There still hadn't been a response to his text, so he sent another. And then he checked the men's restroom, the storage rooms, the closets. He rushed through the kitchen looking for her, asking the employees if they'd seen where she'd gone. While dialing 9-1-1, he questioned the handful of patrons still in the dining area. No one had seen Daisy leave. She'd simply vanished.

FOUR

The man who was shoving a pistol into Daisy's ribs had looked like an easygoing college kid when she'd first seen him.

Young, with stylishly rakish hair and wearing a Dawson University T-shirt with khaki pants, he'd approached Daisy as he'd ambled down the alley appearing to be focused on the screen of his phone. Daisy had seen him coming, but hadn't registered him as a threat. She'd turned her attention to the alley behind him. She'd wanted to do a quick scan of the area to see if by chance the fugitives' truck was hidden back there.

The next thing she knew, she had a gun pressed to her side. The thug draped his arm around her shoulder, making it look to anyone watching like they might be buddies. "Don't scream or I'll drop you right here. I get paid the same whether I bring you back dead or alive," he'd whispered in her ear as she twisted, desperate to loosen his grip on her so she could reach for her gun.

Plastering a big, fake, friendly smile on his face, he'd tightened his grip on her and pulled her back against him. She'd looked into the cold, reptile expression in his eyes and felt a chill pass through her body.

With his gun still trained on her, he let go of her arm for a few seconds as he yanked the gun out of her holster and jammed it into his waistband. Then he grabbed her again.

"What do you want from me?" she demanded.

He didn't answer.

Instead, he resumed pulling her down the alley, laughing and jabbering the whole way about people she'd never heard of, making it appear to anyone who might be looking out onto the alley that the two of them were friends and she was walking with him willingly.

Where was Martin?

The adrenaline pumping through her veins sent her thoughts racing at such breakneck speed that she couldn't determine if it had been minutes or merely seconds since she and this creep had started moving down the alley. But Martin would come looking for her, she was sure of that.

The alley led to a two-lane street where it ended, and then picked up again on the other side. They were moving quickly. She tried to see if the back door of the diner was still in view behind them. But the assailant was strong. He held her close to his side and didn't give her enough room to turn her head.

"Where are you taking me?"

"Shut up," he snapped, with that fake smile still on his face.

The alley was lined with garbage bins pushed up against the backs of the buildings, along with stacks of wooden pallets, recycling bins and empty cardboard boxes. To anyone looking from the back of the diner, Daisy and the jerk holding on to her had probably disappeared almost immediately. Martin might not have any idea where to look for her.

She had to do something to save herself. The alley turned and then ended not too far ahead. There were a few abandoned industrial buildings up there, a rarely used railroad spur surrounded by high weeds and not much else. Maybe the thug intended to force her into a waiting vehicle when they got to the end of the alley. Or maybe he planned to kill her.

This abduction *had* to be related to Daisy's search for Daltrey and Bunker. She was sure of it. University Guy was possibly another hit man who worked for the same Miami mob.

He started to pull her across the street, heading toward the spot where the alley picked back up on the other side. Halfway across the road, she made her body go limp, bending her knees and dropping to the pavement. She'd surprised him, and she slipped out of his grip.

Cars passed by on the main street paralleling the alley just a few yards away. There were people walking on the sidewalk over there. She just needed to somehow get moving in that direction, taking the chance that this criminal wouldn't shoot her when they were in clear view of potential witnesses. As soon as she was beyond his reach, she'd grab her phone and call for help.

She'd landed on her side when she hit the street, and now she moved her hands and knees so that she could push her body up off the asphalt. The skin on her back crawled as she anticipated the blast and pain of a gunshot. At the same time, she fought to focus her thoughts enough for a quick prayer that someone over on the main street would see her and come to help. Maybe that would scare the thug away. Get him to cut his losses and leave before a crowd formed or the cops showed up.

She hoped that slowing down their movement away from the diner like this would give Martin time to find her, slap a pair of cuffs on the kidnapper and get whatever information he could out of him regarding the whereabouts of Daltrey and Bunker before the cops arrived and hauled him to jail.

None of those things happened. Instead, the thug cursed, grabbed her arm and yanked her up off the pavement.

Her hand shot out as she tried to grab the gun he'd taken from her and tucked into his waistband, but he knocked her palm aside before she could reach it. She opened her mouth to scream and he slapped her with the gun in his hand, the extra weight of it sending a bolt of pain radiating through her jawbone.

Stunned by the assault, she was unable to resist as he pulled her the rest of the way across the street and into the alley to a secluded spot behind an industrial garbage can where he threw her to the ground. Her head smacked against the side of a building. She lay there, the alley seeming to swirl as small sparkles of light bounced around the edges of her field of vision.

Do not pass out, she commanded herself, fighting the temptation to close her eyes, block out the dizziness and rest for just a few seconds.

She heard a faint ringing sound, but her addled mind didn't place what was happening until she felt the cold steel of a knife blade the assailant had pulled from a sheath biting her skin from her shoulder across to a point just below her collarbone.

"You're thinking I won't shoot you with so many people within earshot," the kidnapper said, crouching down in front of her, his breath hot and clammy against the side of her face. "Maybe you're right. But there's more than one way to shut you up." He held the wicked-looking knife in front of her face. "You pull a stupid stunt like you did in the street again, and the next cut will be across your throat."

He tucked the knife away, then pulled a phone out of his pocket and tapped the screen. "I've got her," he said into the phone after someone apparently answered on the other end. "We're almost there."

"Get up," he commanded Daisy after disconnecting his call.

While she fumbled around trying to get to her feet, he grabbed her phone from her pocket and yanked the cuffs and pepper spray off her belt.

Frustrated by her own clumsy movements, Daisy bit back on the temptation to fight against him. Right now that would only make things worse. If she waited for a minute or two, the dizziness would hopefully stop and that would be her opportunity to take smart, effective action.

He dragged her along with him to the end of the alley and an old redbrick industrial building. The windows were boarded up and it looked like it had been vacant for years. They walked around to a rusty side door. He pulled it open and shoved her inside.

After the phone call she overheard, she'd expected

to see Daltrey and Bunker waiting, but neither one was there. It didn't look or sound like anyone at all was there. And even though from the outside the building had appeared abandoned, inside it was clear that at least part of it was still being used. They'd walked into what must have been the break room back when there was still a working company housed here. There was a large table in the room, chairs around it, a sink and a couple of working light fixtures that had been left turned on. A door hung open, showing a shadowy hallway that led farther into the building.

"What is this place?" she asked, while scanning, looking for something she could use as a weapon. Her mind was starting to clear. She could see packaging materials on the counter. Plastic bags. Tape. And something that might be a digital scale. Was this a drug distribution center? Or some kind of clearinghouse where other illegal or stolen items could be shipped out of the area?

And what would this have to do with her pursuit of Daltrey and Bunker? Did their mob cohorts have criminal ties to Jameson that local law enforcement did not yet know about?

The kidnapper flung her into a plastic chair, snatched up a roll of duct tape from the counter and taped her wrists together behind her back.

"You don't have to do this," she said. She had no idea what he planned to do, but she could imagine several things, all of them terrifying.

He tore off another strip of duct tape and slapped it over her mouth. When she started to scream, he slapped another piece over the first, this one covering part of her nose. It was hard to breathe. He yanked her up out of the chair, dragged her across the room where he opened the door of a storage closet and shoved her inside and slammed the door shut.

She fell and hit her head against the back wall. The dizzy sensation she'd had earlier came roaring back. Panic, like a wild animal trapped behind her rib cage, thrashed around in her chest.

She heard the thug talking on a phone, the volume turned up loud enough that she could hear some of the words spoken by the person on the other end. They were talking about prices, about payment and taking care of their other problem, whatever that was.

Heart racing with fear, she was breathing hard, or trying to, but the tape over her mouth and part of her nose wouldn't let her draw in enough breath. She started to feel suffocated, like she was going to pass out.

The voice on the other end of the call began to sound familiar to her. A mental image of Daltrey and Bunker at the shopping mall drifted into her mind, and she realized it was Ivan Bunker on the other end of the call.

The kidnapper started to shout, saying something about sticking his neck out and taking all the risks. Feeling even more like she was about to pass out, Daisy couldn't follow the thread of the conversation. She heard another, different voice start yelling, but the sound was muffled. It took her a few seconds to realize the voice belonged to someone else here in the building, and that it sounded familiar. She strained to listen, hoping it was Martin. But it wasn't.

So who was it?

She was still trying to figure out the answer as her oxygen-deprived brain spiraled into darkness.

"The truck Daltrey and Bunker were last seen driving was found abandoned near the campgrounds out at Pearce Park about an hour ago," Sergeant Ken Cruise said to Martin. "We have no idea what they're driving right now, but we've contacted all the car rental businesses in town and we're also paying close attention to stolen vehicle reports in hopes of finding them."

Martin nodded, his mind racing as he tried to think of what he could do to find Daisy. His initial assumption was that Daltrey and Bunker had grabbed her in the alley, thrown her into their vehicle and raced away. Hearing the news that no one knew what the two fugitives were driving, so the police would have no idea what they were looking for, had nearly broken his heart.

"Video feeds." He impatiently barked the words at Cruise, a Jameson cop whom Martin had worked with on previous cases. "There's got to be video from the businesses around here that we can view. And what about people here in the restaurant?" He gestured at the patrons in the diner. "You can't let them leave without being interviewed. Somebody *has* to have seen something."

Patrol cars were continuing to arrive at the diner, both from the Jameson PD and Beckett County Sheriff's Department.

Martin strode out the back door into the alley, thinking maybe this time he'd see something he'd missed before that would give him an idea about what had happened, which way the person or people who'd grabbed Daisy had gone, *something*. Cruise walked beside him, talking on his collar mic, directing a couple of units to begin patrolling through the neighborhood.

"In the aftermath of the shoot-out at the Acorn Valley Mall, everybody in law enforcement in the surrounding four states knows what Daltrey and Bunker look like. And most cops in the county know what Daisy looks like. We know who we're searching for. Even without knowing what kind of vehicle she might be riding in, we can find her."

A patrol car moved down the alley. This was the oldest part of town and businesses along the street had been added slowly, over time, and before there was much in the way of city planning. As a result, the alley was not exactly a straight line. You couldn't stand in one spot and see the whole length of it. Plus, the various trash cans and stacks of recyclables, not to mention delivery containers and pallets out here, didn't help. Streets intersected the alley in both directions. And all of the businesses had back doors. Someone could have just grabbed Daisy and yanked her into any one of the buildings.

Martin had already jogged a short distance in each direction looking for Daisy while he'd been on the line with the 9-1-1 operator, but he'd gotten no indication of which way she'd gone. Mentally, he was kicking himself for not staying by her side. He knew that wallowing in regret right now wasn't productive, but it threatened to overwhelm his thoughts, nevertheless.

"We don't know what happened, but I'm going to start with the theory that her disappearance is related to Beau Daltrey and Ivan Bunker, because that seems likely," the sergeant said. "Tell me, how would they have known where Daisy was? And why do you think they'd have chosen to come out of hiding to grab her right now?"

"We thought Daltrey and Bunker might have a connection to this area so we started asking around," Martin answered. "We must have struck a nerve somewhere. I guess the hit men were watching us and we didn't notice." And that realization was another reason Martin wanted to kick himself.

"What businesses did you visit while you were canvassing the neighborhood?"

Martin impatiently rattled off the names while Cruise jotted them down.

Over the sergeant's radio, Martin heard a sheriff's deputy with a K-9 reporting their arrival on scene at the diner.

"Do you have anything with Daisy's scent on it?" the sergeant asked.

"Let me look in my truck." *Please Lord, let Daisy have left something there*, Martin prayed silently as he dashed through the diner, where uniformed officers were questioning the patrons, and out the front door. He ran past the police dog handler and her K-9 and raced down the street to his parked truck. He yanked open the door and spotted a pair of knit gloves she'd worn earlier in the day when the air was still chilly.

He hurried back to the diner and then out the back door to the alley exit where the sergeant, dog handler and the barking, excited K-9 were waiting.

He gave the gloves to the handler, who held them out for her dog to smell and was somehow able to communicate to the animal that Martin, despite his scent being on the gloves, was not the person they were tracking. After a few whiffs, the canine started moving eastward down the alley. The dog pulled forward at the end of a long leather leash, whining with impatient excitement. The handler, Martin and Sergeant Cruise followed.

Martin had gotten what he'd desperately wanted—a lead on which direction to look. But at the same time, he couldn't help dreading what they might end up finding. The hit men had already murdered Jimmy Nestor at the rec hall. Authorities in Miami had been in the process of charging Daltrey and Bunker with murder when they jumped bail. Martin and Daisy must have been close to finding them this morning. Daisy was a talented, determined tracker with her finger on the pulse of her town. The fugitives had a lot to gain by her death, and not much reason to keep her alive.

The K-9 led them down the twists and turns of the alley, crossed the street and kept going on the other side. The dog headed to a spot behind an industrial trash container where there were drops of blood. Martin's heart fell to his feet.

The sergeant keyed his radio and directed a couple of his officers to meet with them in the east end of the alley.

Martin barely had time to recover from the fear that had sent his pulse pounding in his ears when the dog yelped and took off again, trotting toward a dilapidated building with covered windows.

The large loading-dock doors that faced the alley were locked into place. The cops fanned around the building, covering all sides, while the dog pulled insis-

tently toward a side door. The sergeant tested the door
and found it unlocked. He drew his pistol and officers
were put into place beside him with long guns.

Because Martin wasn't a law enforcement officer, he
was ordered to move back and wait until the cops made
entry. As soon as the officers made entry, and didn't
face resistance, he followed them through the door. He
saw an overturned chair, a few items on the counter and
nothing more. Daisy was nowhere in sight. The weight
of disappointment nearly crushed him.

But then the dog pulled its handler toward a door
that looked like it led to a closet. When Cruise opened
the door, Martin was right behind him. He saw Daisy,
crumpled on the floor, moaning and barely conscious.
He dropped to his knees and prayed, "Please, Lord, let
her be alive," as he pulled thick tape from her mouth
and nose.

She gasped and began to thrash around. He put his
arm under her shoulders and knees, lifted her and carried her out into the room, where he gently set her down
on the floor and saw the blood on her shirt for the first
time. He heard Cruise behind him calling for an ambulance. Meanwhile, Martin leaned down and pressed
his cheek against hers, holding her hand while speaking
softly into her ear, telling her that he was there, that she
was safe and that he would take care of her.

He felt her eyelashes flutter against his cheek. Seconds later she sucked in a deep breath, opened her eyes
and started mumbling something about her mom.

There was no telling what Daisy had been through
in the ninety minutes since she'd disappeared from the
diner. The trauma must have her trapped in some kind

of waking nightmare. "I'm here with you," Martin repeated, thinking she was calling for her mom because she'd forgotten that Shannon had been kidnapped.

Hissing her frustration, Daisy grabbed a fistful of the front of Martin's shirt and struggled to sit up. "I'm trying to tell you that my mother is *here*," she rasped. "I heard her."

Martin glanced at the sergeant. The cops hadn't done a sweep of the entire building, yet.

"Just listen for a minute," Daisy said, "and you'll hear her, too."

Cruise signaled to the other officers to stand still and be quiet.

Martin could hear a faint voice. He glanced at Cruise, who nodded in return. He'd heard it, too.

Martin and the K-9 handler waited with Daisy, while Cruise and another officer cautiously started down the dark hallway and were soon out of sight. Martin squeezed Daisy's hand, afraid to wrap his arm around her shoulder again now that he knew it was injured. He heard the sound of a door being broken down, and then he heard Shannon Lopez's voice.

Daisy burst into tears of relief, and Martin almost did, too. Moments later, Mrs. Lopez hurried down the hall, calling out, "Daisy? Are you here? Is it true?" She stepped into the room, pale and bruised and a little unsteady on her feet.

"Mom!" Daisy held out her arms toward her.

Shannon's gaze fixed on the blood on Daisy's shirt, and her steps faltered. "Honey, what happened?"

"I'll be okay, Mom," Daisy said, impatiently waving the arms she was still holding out toward her mother.

Shannon dropped down so that she could wrap her arms around her daughter. "Thank You, Lord," she said over and over. "Thank You."

"Amen," Martin said.

Hearing him, Mrs. Lopez reached for Martin and gave him a hug, as well.

Cruise gave the two women a few precious minutes to reunite, but then the ambulance arrived. He insisted that both women be transported to the hospital, but he wanted to talk to them before they left.

Daisy told him about the abduction and relayed the snippets of phone conversation she'd overheard as she'd drifted in and out of consciousness while locked in the closet. "It sounded like the thug who grabbed me was paid by Ivan Bunker to do it." She glanced at her mom. "I think they paid him to keep Mom here, too. He talked to Bunker about getting paid for *other business*. I don't know if this guy is connected to the mob they worked for down in Florida, or if he's just some criminal low-life that was willing to help them out. At some point, I heard him tell someone that the cops were getting close and that he 'isn't going to prison for nobody.'"

"So that's probably when he left," the sergeant said.

A paramedic and EMT came into the room and moved toward Daisy and her mother.

"Mom, are you okay?" Daisy asked. "I'm so sorry I got you into this."

"Stop that," Mrs. Lopez said, reaching over to brush her daughter's hair out of her eyes. "This is not your fault. And I'm proud of you for going after criminals and bringing them to justice."

Sergeant Cruise asked several questions as the EMT

started taking Shannon's vital signs and the paramedic examined the wound on Daisy's shoulder.

As it turned out, Shannon had had no idea that Daisy was in the building when she'd initially started hollering for help. She'd just been able to hear that someone was there and she'd called out in desperation. After the shoot-out at the mall, she'd been shuttled around as the criminals tried to evade the police before she was brought here and locked in a small windowless office. The kidnappers had given her food and water, so she was in decent health. But she'd been under no illusions about the fate they had planned for her.

Cruise cut short his interview for now, so the women could get medical treatment. But he wanted to question them both further as soon as they were cleared by a doctor.

"I'm so glad we found you," Daisy said. "At least this nightmare is over."

Tears filled Shannon's eyes. "Oh, honey, I wish that were so." She sighed deeply. "I heard the men who kidnapped me talking to someone on the phone. From their tone, it sounded like the person they were talking to was their boss. I knew they meant to kill me, because they didn't seem to care what I overheard." She wiped the tears from her eyes and reached for Daisy's hands and gave them a squeeze before letting go. "The person they were talking to said they have to kill you. They have to do it to send a message to anyone paying attention that they can handle you so that their criminal syndicate doesn't look weak."

Martin looked at Daisy and prayed quietly, "Lord, please don't let that happen."

FIVE

"It's true, you can't keep a good woman down," Sheriff Russell said to Daisy as she stepped into the examining room at Beckett County Hospital with her Stetson hat in her hand. She glanced around and offered a nod of acknowledgment to Martin, Shannon and Daisy's aunt Jessica, who were also jammed into the small room.

Daisy raised her hand in a half-hearted greeting. She was sitting on the edge of the examining table, dressed in clean clothes that Millie had packed and had Alvis drop off at the hospital for her. She was swinging her feet a little bit, feeling impatient and ready to get back to work.

Five hours had passed since she'd been rescued at the warehouse. She was cranky and had a pounding headache. And she was more determined than ever to find Beau Daltrey and Ivan Bunker and get them locked up. Part of her wanted to go after the jerk in the alley who'd grabbed her and taken her hostage. But he was not a bail jumper and tracking him wasn't her job. That was for the police to take care of. Still, she couldn't help imagining doing it herself.

"Have you found the creep who kidnapped me?" she asked the sheriff.

"Not yet. He'd broken into that building, had no legal right to be there or utilities connected, so we can't identify him that way. Based on your description, sheriff's deputies and Jameson Police patrol officers are out looking for him. Most likely he has a criminal record, so by morning we should have some mug shots for you to look over."

"I'll know him when I see him, believe me." Daisy's professional ego was bruised by the fact that she'd been overtaken by a single assailant. Later, she would go over every detail of what had happened multiple times, taking away every possible lesson to make sure that never happened again. The only other thing she could do was identify the kidnapper, testify against him in court and make sure he went to prison where he belonged so he couldn't hurt anybody else.

The sheriff glanced at Daisy's shoulder. "How many stitches did you need?"

"None." She shook her head, felt a little queasy and immediately stopped. "The cut wasn't deep enough to do any serious damage, so they just taped it up. And they checked out my head. No major damage there."

"That's what you say," Martin teased.

He was trying to lighten the mood, because that's what Martin did. People who didn't know him well thought he was a simple, unfettered, easygoing guy. Daisy knew better. Yes, he was those things. But he was also more. Martin watched the people around him, paid attention to how they felt and what they cared about. He read a lot and was interested in many things. But he kept a lot of that hidden, letting only bits and pieces slip out occasionally in conversation. Daisy thought it might be due to his verbally abusive father and critical, sarcastic mother. She'd interacted with both of them a few times over the years, and each time, within minutes, she'd found herself silently giving thanks in prayer that Martin's great-aunt and -uncle had stepped into his life when they did, showing him love and acceptance and leading him to faith. They had done a lot for him, but there were still emotional knots inside him that were tight, and he wasn't willing to let Daisy, or anyone else, apparently, ease them.

"Honey, if he's trying to say you have a hard head, he's right," Shannon said to Daisy. "And that's turned out to be a good thing." Shannon Lopez laughed and walked over to Martin to give him a hug. One of many she'd given him over the afternoon, along with multiple offers of thanks for alerting police so she and her daughter could be rescued.

Martin had accomplished what he'd set out to do: taken a dark moment and made it a little lighter.

Seeing her mom with Martin brought back a lot of memories of good times over the years when Martin had come to the house to hang out with Aaron, and later to visit Daisy and her mom. Barbecues, holiday gatherings, lazy afternoons spent fishing at one of the local lakes. She'd felt that spark of attraction each time she'd seen him over the last year or so. But he'd never seemed to feel the same way. It had hurt then when he hadn't responded the way she'd wanted him to and it stung now. Which was dumb, because she'd already given up on

Martin feeling the same way she did. About a hundred times, or so it sometimes seemed.

"This is my aunt Jessica," Daisy said to the sheriff, making the introduction between the two women in an attempt to shift her thoughts away from Martin. "My mom's going to be staying with her for a while." Shannon had spent several hours with law enforcement today, detailing how she'd been kidnapped from her front yard and later, after the shoot-out at the mall, had been taken to the abandoned industrial building and locked up.

The sheriff nodded. "Nice to meet you."

Shannon didn't have any significant physical injuries from her ordeal and that was good news, but Daisy knew her mom was bound to experience some emotional fallout in the aftermath of all that had happened once she had a few quiet moments to process everything. Being with her sister, Jessica, would be good for her. This would not be a good time for her mom to stay home alone.

An employee from the hospital's administration office walked into the room with some information for Daisy to look over and acknowledgments for her to sign.

"I'm going to head home to my apartment as soon as I finish with this," Daisy said to her mom. "You and Aunt Jessica might as well head on out of here. Get some rest. I'll call you first thing in the morning." She clasped her hands in front of her. "Have you told Aaron about any of this yet?"

Shannon looked away for a moment, then turned her gaze to Daisy. "I have not. I was thinking it might be best to wait a little longer, maybe even until all the bad guys are captured. I don't want to upset him when there's nothing he can do."

"I was thinking the same thing." Daisy blew out a sigh of relief. "But you know, when we do tell him, he's going to be annoyed that we waited."

Shannon shrugged her shoulder and flashed a grin. "I'm the mom. I don't care how big he is, *he* is not telling *me* what I should do."

After kisses and hugs, with everyone being careful of Daisy's injured shoulder, Shannon and Jessica left.

"Are you sure you don't want to stay with your aunt, too?" Sheriff Russell asked after they were gone. "According to what your mother overheard, you've got a mob hit out on you now. That's no small thing. Maybe you need to hide somewhere for a while."

"There's a good chance that somehow they'd find me there. I don't want to bring danger to my mom and my aunt and my aunt's family." She told the sheriff about her paid informants at the convenience store and hair salon behaving strangely and refusing to help her. "At first I couldn't figure out what was going on. But now I'm starting to get the picture. I'm thinking Daltrey and Bunker have mob money to spread around in town to get them the help they need."

"And they might be threatening people who normally help you. But how would they know who those people were?"

Daisy crossed her arms over her chest. "That's something I haven't figured out, yet. All I know is my mom is safer away from me, and I'm safest with armed bounty hunters." She looked to Martin for reassurance before she realized what she was doing. He held her gaze and nodded, giving her the sense of comfort that she craved right now. And then she felt that spark, that something-more-than-friendship feeling. She couldn't get away from it even though she really wanted to.

The sheriff nodded. "Where you stay is your decision to make. I'd probably make the same one. We'll be following up on the information you gave Sergeant Cruise earlier today. And we'll get the security video from Your Family Store and see if Daltrey or Bunker did go in there to buy a burner phone. If they did, we might be able to get some useful information. The clerk who rang them up could have noticed something helpful. Maybe we'll be able to see them meet up with someone else inside the store.

"We'll get a record on the calls on the pay phone at Rizzoli's, too. I don't expect that to help us find the bad guys in the short term, but if we can find proof of conversations between them and other members of their crime syndicate while they were fugitives from justice, that might help with substantial organized crime prosecutions later."

"When you're on the hunt for somebody, you never know which small detail will ultimately lead you to the capture," Martin said.

The sheriff nodded. "Agreed." She tapped her hat lightly against her leg. "I need to get back to work. We're stretched a little thin with everything going on right now." To Daisy she said, "I'm glad to see you're doing all right. Get some rest."

The sheriff said her goodbyes and left. And the admin got everything taken care of that she needed for Daisy to be released. A few minutes after she left, an orderly arrived with a wheelchair to take Daisy out of the hospital. Martin went to pull his truck up to the front entrance, then he hopped out and held her arm, ignoring her protests that she could do it on her own as she moved from the wheelchair to the passenger seat of his truck.

It was dark outside now, and fall was most definitely in the air. Moving from the warmth of the hospital into the cold outside had Daisy shivering until the air blowing out of the vents inside Martin's truck finally heated up and took the edge off. Outside, the chill breeze sent dried leaves cartwheeling across the parking lot.

"Here." Martin reached into the glove box, pulled out Daisy's phone and handed it to her. "This was recovered at the warehouse. The jerk who grabbed you probably has your gun. It wasn't found on the scene. Same with your pepper spray and cuffs."

"Thank you." The phone battery was dead and the screen was cracked. She plugged it into a charging cord on the truck's console. It immediately started chiming with notifications.

"How about we turn that off for right now?" Martin said, taking a good look around before pulling away from the parking lot and into traffic. "Let your brain rest a little bit."

Martin cared about her, Daisy reminded herself. He looked out for her. He was here right now when she needed him most. Shouldn't that be enough?

She glanced over at his profile, visible in the light from the truck's control panel and from the widely spaced streetlights they passed under on their way to the bail bond office. He had sharp, aquiline features and deep-set dark eyes. He might look intimidating to anyone who didn't know him. At least until he flashed that boyish smile that always tempted her to smile back. Even when she didn't want to.

She was stuck between two worlds when it came to Martin. She couldn't turn off her feelings for him, and she couldn't possibly give up their friendship in the hope that that would help her let go and move on.

"You're right. I think ignoring my phone for a bit might be a good idea." The people she was most concerned with hearing from would know that she was with Martin, and would contact him if there was an important reason they needed to talk to her. She powered off her phone while it continued to charge.

"Wait, did you just admit I was right about something?" Martin teased. "Let me hit the record button on my phone and say that again. Just so I can preserve the memory."

Daisy rolled her eyes, even though she knew he couldn't see her, and hid a grin as she glanced at the side mirror to see if they were being followed. Martin made a few random turns, also keeping an eye out for anyone trailing them. It wasn't a secret that she worked and lived at the bail bonds office, but there was no reason to make it easy for anyone to find her precise location right now.

She glanced over at Martin again and saw that he'd quietly taken his gun out of his holster and placed it on the seat beside him where he could grab it in an instant. True to form, even when he was joking with her, he was also serious and aware of the situation around him. The combination could be frustrating and fascinating.

And she knew that leaning into him emotionally, relying on him for comfort and strength, would come with a price. She would pay it when all of this was over and they went their separate ways. But for right now, what other choice did she have?

She had bad guys to capture. And apparently these guys weren't just going to try to avoid being captured by Daisy and skip town, like normal fugitives. They were going to try to kill her first.

Martin called Millie while he and Daisy were still a few miles out to let her know that they would be arriving outside the office's back door shortly and to verify the office was secure and there were no clients in the building. He wasn't taking any chances with Daisy's safety. Millie told him there weren't any customers in the building and that she and Alvis would immediately do a check of the entire building and double-check the locks on the exterior doors. With professional mob hit men coming after Daisy, they couldn't be too careful.

Her assurances should have made Martin feel better, but they didn't. Not because he doubted Millie, but because Daisy could have very easily been killed today. Or yesterday, for that matter, when bullets were flying in her direction on two different occasions. She had chosen a risky occupation for her life's work. She had every right to do so, and the fact was, she was good at it. But the situation now was entirely different from anything she'd faced before.

This bounty hunt had started on the assumption that Beau Daltrey and Ivan Bunker had come to Montana because they thought it would be easy to hide here and it offered the additional benefit of being a long way from their home base in Miami. Now, it was looking like the situation was more complicated than that. The hit men apparently had a support network in Jameson. How could a Miami mob organization have a presence in town and no one in local law enforcement know about it?

Beside him, Daisy continued to keep an eye on the side mirror, watching for anyone tailing them. She was slouched in her seat, with her chin tilted slightly downward and the collar of her jacket pulled up. Like she was hiding. That posture was so unlike Daisy, who was normally on the edge of her seat, bold and ready to take on whatever challenge came her way. The last few days had taken a lot out of her. Understandably. Maybe he could convince her to stay home for a couple of days and rest. Let someone else do part of the legwork to find their two fugitives. He had to trust the cops to find the kidnapper from the alley. Unless it turned out that that slimeball was a bail jumper, too. In which case Martin would be *very* happy to help bring him to justice.

"I'll call Cassie tomorrow morning," Martin said. "Ask her to send Leon and Harry for a couple of days. Adding two more bounty hunters to the party might speed up the capture."

"We don't have any solid leads for them to chase down," Daisy said. "It doesn't make sense to ask them to come until we do. They don't live over here and neither one of them has any kind of an informant network in Jameson. I know that's true because any time they chase somebody over in this direction they ask me for my help."

She had a point.

She rolled down her window to adjust the side mirror, and cool air rushed into the warm truck.

"I'm keeping an eye on the vehicles around us," Martin said. "You seem glued to that mirror. Do you think I'm not doing my job?" he teased.

Actually, Martin was a natural at being vigilant. In the household he grew up in, he never knew when one or both of his parents would be set off by something that aggravated them. Sometimes, their temper seemed to be triggered by absolutely nothing. But if he didn't want to be in the pathway of some object thrown in aggravation, or if he didn't want to get smacked by a grown-up looking to let off a little steam, he needed to pay attention and know when to get out of the way.

"It's not that I don't think you're doing your job," Daisy said. "It's just that you're not as good at it as I am." She turned to him, flashing a slight, sly smile that lifted a heavy weight off his chest. "I am the person who originally trained you to be a bounty hunter, you know."

It was true; his original training had come from helping her track down people when she was just starting out bounty hunting. But he liked to think he might have learned a thing or two on his own since then. There'd always been a bit of a competitive streak between the two of them. It was part of what made it fun to be around her.

They arrived at Peak Bail Bonds and he sent a quick text to Millie letting her know they'd made it. Alvis opened the door for them, standing beside it with a gun in his hand.

"You don't look like you've got much trust in humanity right now," Daisy commented dryly as she walked past him.

Alvis smiled at the comment, but Martin could see that the smile didn't reach the older man's eyes. And instead of looking at Daisy as she walked by, he'd kept his gaze on the dark tree line at the back of the building until everyone was inside and he could close and lock the door.

Millie and Alvis had found out the basic facts of what had happened today when Daisy called asking for some clean clothes to be brought to the hospital.

In the lobby, Millie gave Daisy a light hug, careful of her shoulder injury. "I've sent Justine and Steve home for the day and we've got everything closed up so it'll be nice and quiet. I want you to just go on up and go to bed."

In Martin's opinion, that was exactly what needed to happen.

"I am exhausted," Daisy said. "But before I head up to my apartment, we need to talk."

She walked over to her desk in the office area and dropped down heavily into her chair. Martin felt his neck and shoulders tense with worry that she was going to push herself too hard as he followed her over in that direction, along with Millie and Alvis.

"I realize that you generally know what happened to me today," she said to Millie and Alvis. "But what you might not know is the Miami mob that Daltrey and Bunker are connected with has put an assassination hit order on me."

The couple's faces, which had already looked concerned, immediately turned pale.

"I don't know if that means only Daltrey and Bunker have been ordered to kill me, if there are other mob-connected people in town who will be attempting to kill me or if the mob is looking to hire local freelancers to do the job. I have earned my share of criminal enemies over the years, so they probably wouldn't have much trouble finding someone who is willing to help them."

Even though this wasn't news to Martin, her words, spoken in a tired, monotone voice, turned his blood cold.

"This new development places everyone around me in a very dangerous position. Especially you, since I live and work in your building." She cleared her throat. "If you want me to leave, I understand. The last thing I want to do is put you in any danger. And don't worry, I have places to go."

Like North Star Ranch, Martin thought. That was the horse ranch in Idaho where his boss, Cassie, lived. People had gone there for protection before.

Alvis crossed his arms over his chest. "Don't be ridiculous," he said, his voice gravelly. "You're staying here."

Millie nodded forcefully, her graying curls bouncing on her shoulders. "He's right. We decided a long time ago that we weren't going to let bad people intimidate us out of doing good."

"Thank you." Daisy's voice sounded whispery, and almost as if she was going to cry.

Which made Martin feel like he could cry. Daisy was tough. If she was nearing her breaking point, she was really hurting.

She gestured toward the laptop on her desk. "Tomorrow I want to make sure I've got my entire confidential informant list updated. And then I want to start talking to some of the informants, find out who leaned on them and told them not to talk to me." She glanced at Martin. "And I'm going to start with Louis at QuickStop."

"You sure you don't want to take a break for a few days first?" Martin asked her.

"That would give the bad guys time to rest up, too," Daisy said. "Maybe regroup and get better organized. That would put us all in greater danger. No, I want to keep the pressure on them so they're too busy looking over their shoulder to plan an attack."

Yeah, Martin wasn't going to be able to talk her into hiding out at the ranch. No way.

She stood up a little unsteadily. "Okay, now I'm ready to go lie down for a while."

Martin hurried over to wrap an arm around her and help her up the stairs. Alvis and Millie followed.

While Alvis and Millie continued up toward their third-floor apartment, and the excited yips of their homely rescue puppy, Martin walked Daisy into her apartment and had a quick look around. Just to be sure it was safe.

She looked so tired that he resisted the temptation to sit down on her small sofa and keep her company for a while. Because really, he'd be doing it for himself. Instead, he wrapped an arm around her good shoulder and pulled her as close as he dared. When she dropped her head down to the base of his neck, her warm breath light against the surface of his skin, he felt a lump in his throat. He knew that despite her bravado, she was scared. He was scared, too.

He waited until she pulled away from him before he said good-night. He stepped into the hallway and made sure she locked her door after he closed it behind him.

He kept his own door open so he could hear if anyone walked down the hallway outside her apartment. They were dealing with professional assassins. Anything was possible. And he had no doubt that the dangerous situation Daisy had been facing over the last couple of days was going to get worse.

SIX

"This is him. This is the man who grabbed me in the alley."

Martin leaned over Daisy's shoulder to get a better look as she tapped the mug shot of a narrow-faced man, in his late twenties or early thirties, with a wispy goatee. The guy didn't look at all familiar to him.

"So who is he?" Daisy asked, pointing at the photo while shifting her gaze from the tablet screen to the cop standing on the other side of the table. "What's his name?"

As promised, the sheriff, as head of the joint task force with the police department, had made certain there was an array of mug shots for Daisy to look at first thing this morning. Martin had tried to get Daisy to allow the cops to come to the bail bond office with their photos so that she could stay home and continue recovering from yesterday's ordeal, but she had insisted they come here to the sheriff's department office. Her reasoning had been that any time they spent in one of the law enforcement offices offered the chance to see or overhear something that could help them in their pursuit of Daltrey and Bunker.

Detective Stu Gerber, who'd taken over the case, reached for the tablet and pulled it toward him, nodding to himself. "This would be Tony Valens. He's been arrested for drug possession and possession with intent to sell several times down in Missoula. Did some time in lockup, then surfaced here about a year ago. He's a known associate of a couple of dealers we've busted, but we haven't had any solid reason to grab him and lock him up. Until now."

Gerber called a deputy into the room and showed her the tablet. "Tony Valens."

"All right, I'll send this out to all the patrol units right now. Then I'll look up his last known address so we can move on him." The deputy gave Daisy and Martin a brief nod of acknowledgment before turning on her heel and leaving.

"So you know where to find him?" Daisy asked.

"He probably didn't go home after he grabbed you and then fled the scene at the industrial building," the detective said. "Although you never know, offenders have done stranger things. But based on his criminal record and known associates, we'll have some places to start looking. And then there's the digital trail we can follow as soon as we track down his phone." He nodded. "We've got a good chance of finding him."

Martin's heart started to beat a little faster, prodded by the hope that the quick capture of Valens would lead to the recovery of Daltrey and Bunker. At which point this nightmare would be over and Daisy would finally be safe.

Gerber sat down at the table and tapped out something on his tablet.

Impatient to have all of this wrapped up and over with, Martin remained standing. What he wanted to do was go out with the deputies who were—hopefully—about to bust Tony Valens. But that, of course, was not possible. And he reminded himself that the law officers were perfectly capable of doing their job without him. He just wished he could be there to help.

"Do you have any idea how Valens is connected to Daltrey and Bunker?" Martin asked. "Or any idea how Valens could be connected to the mob in general?"

Gerber finished what he was doing on his tablet, looked up and then leaned back in his chair. "There's nothing specific in his record that points to any connection to organized crime. The main reasons we put him in the photo lineup are that he fit the physical description and he's a known criminal. We suspect he's dealing drugs in Jameson, but we haven't been able to prove it. He's got to have some kind of connections to get his product, but the idea of a big-time Miami organized crime syndicate having a connection to Jameson, Montana, is hard to believe. It's unsettling to think they could have a presence here without us knowing about it. But maybe that is the source of his drugs."

"Maybe all of this started recently," Daisy said, her voice fainter than usual.

Martin glanced over and saw her rubbing her shirt around the spot where she'd been cut yesterday. When they were having coffee this morning she'd mentioned it was starting to itch. And then he'd suggested that it was too soon for her to get back to work and she should just stay home. He'd gotten a loud sigh and an eye roll from her for his efforts.

"Maybe Daltrey and Bunker started that connection. We know they were nearly captured while they were hiding in Atlanta before they disappeared from there eight weeks ago," she added. "If they came straight here when they skipped out of Georgia, eight weeks would be enough time to get a good start on an illegal business if they knew what they were doing."

"What information have you gotten from researching the warehouse?" Martin asked. "Did you get a name for the person leasing the place or requesting that the utilities be connected? Anything like that?"

"The building is owned by an investment company in Portland," the detective said. "No one leased it from them so it should be vacant. The structural integrity as well as electrical systems don't meet code for occupancy, so they haven't had it on the market trying to attract tenants. It looks like our kidnapper broke into the place, brought in a battery-operated generator and hauled in some bottled water. There's no sign that he actually lived there, so I'm guessing he used it to receive and then repackage drugs for resale."

"And he used it for locking up people," Daisy muttered.

Martin glanced at her. She was looking pale. He wanted to get her out of here, soon.

"How is your mother?" the detective asked.

"I talked to her this morning. She's okay, mostly worried about me." Daisy smiled. "You probably know how that is."

Gerber, who was perhaps a couple of years older than Martin, smiled at her in return. "Yes, I do."

"So what are you doing right now?" Martin snapped,

feeling a stab of jealousy that he absolutely did not want to deal with at all. "We don't have time for chitchat."

Daisy gave him a wide-eyed look.

"I've sent out notifications and emails while we've been talking," the detective said smoothly. "Deputies are already en route to Valens's last known address. Jameson police and the sheriff's department will be on the lookout for him. And we already have people starting to track his digital trail."

The detective stood, indicating that their meeting was over. Martin and Daisy also got to their feet.

"What do you two plan to do next?" Gerber asked.

Martin glanced at Daisy. She was definitely fading. "We're going back to the office to do some research," he said. "Find out if the Carters ever posted bail for Tony Valens. Or see if they could get information out of anybody in their bail bonds network of friends down in Missoula."

They said their goodbyes, and Martin stayed close as he and Daisy walked outside. He scanned the surroundings carefully as they walked to his truck. The area just outside the sheriff's department main headquarters ought to be secure, but he wasn't taking any chances. There was no telling the size of the criminal network in Jameson that was willing to work with or for Daltrey and Bunker and their mob bosses. Attacks on Daisy could happen anywhere, at any time.

Daisy sat at her desk in front of a laptop computer and squeezed the thick handle of her empty coffee mug, willing herself to stay awake and alert.

There'd been freshly brewed coffee in the glass ca-

rafe in the office when she and Martin arrived back at
the Peak Bail Bonds office. She'd filled three-quarters
of a mug with coffee, dumped in a lot of cold milk
to cool it down so she could drink it faster and then
squirted in a healthy dose of chocolate syrup for a de-
licious flavor and a sugar kick. It was her go-to drink
when she was working a challenging case and she
needed some quick energy to keep her going. So far
this morning, it wasn't helping.

Daisy and Martin were with Alvis and Millie in the
back part of the office, where a jutting section of wall
kept them out of view of anyone in the lobby. There
was, however, a section of two-way mirror in that wall
so that anyone back there could see into the lobby without being seen.

Justine and Steve were parked at the front counter.
The front door was locked, but high flight-risk clients
out on bail were allowed through the door to do their re-
quired in-person check-ins. New bonds were still being
written, and the skip-tracing work Justine specialized in
was still being conducted. They were still open for business, but everyone was being careful. Alvis and Millie
had offered to close the place down for a few days to
help Daisy feel safe, but she'd insisted they keep things
running. She knew their offer was sincere, but she also
knew they couldn't afford to put a freeze on doing business. They needed an income like anyone else.

Still, the feeling in the office was more than a little
bit tense.

"Tony Valens is not someone we've written bail on,"
Millie said, looking through a pair of half-glasses at
the screen of the laptop sitting on her desk. "I'll check

with our bail bonds friends in Missoula and see if they have anything."

"I don't see him mentioned in our contact database," Daisy said, closing the file. She did a quick check on her email and saw that Deputy Gerber had sent her a mug shot of Valens. She opened the file and clicked to print a few copies of the photo in case she needed it later to show to people around town. She carried one of the printouts over to Millie to show her.

"He doesn't look familiar," Millie said, shaking her head. "Send me that photo. I'll add him to our contact database."

Along with information on their clients, Peak Bail Bonds maintained a pretty extensive database of clients' known associates, as well as the names of people bounty hunters had come in contact with while tracking bail jumpers, and people who were out and about in the community, saw things going on and were willing to share information or keep an eye out for an offender in return for payment.

"Tony Valens doesn't look familiar to me, either," Alvis said. He'd walked over from his desk to take a look.

Daisy sent the photo file to Millie, copying in Martin and Alvis.

"Okay, I've got some basics on him," Justine said. The red-haired single mom in her late thirties had taught herself the basics of skip tracing while trying to track down her ex-husband for child support payments. She rattled off Valens's date of birth, criminal convictions and last known address.

"I'm sure the cops are sitting on that address if they haven't found him there already," Alvis said.

The buzzer at the front door sounded and Daisy nearly jumped out of her skin. Martin, who'd been leaning against the nearby wall with his arms crossed, straightened up and moved his hand so that it rested near the gun at his side.

"This should be okay," Steve called out from the front counter. "It's Pete Keller here for his daily check-in."

"He's a high flight risk because he's an addict who keeps relapsing," Daisy said to Martin. Still, the fact that he was a familiar face didn't mean that he was safe. If he'd fallen off the wagon again and was in the throes of his addiction, he'd do anything for money to buy drugs. Even take a shot at Daisy if her fugitives' criminal network had somehow gotten a hold on him.

Heart racing in her chest and finding it a little bit hard to breathe, Daisy watched through the two-way mirror as Steve walked to the door, opened it, spoke to Pete and then closed and locked the door.

She blew out her breath, and then realized that everyone else in the office had also stopped what they were doing to watch. Learning that they were dealing with a criminal force bigger than just Daltrey and Bunker was unnerving. Daisy was pretty certain she wasn't the only one still processing that new fact.

"I've found a couple of previous employers for Valens, too," Justine added.

"The cops will be on that," Martin said. "But it might be worth talking to his former coworkers and neighbors after the police are done."

"Agreed," Daisy said. There were plenty of people

who would not help the cops for a variety of reasons. But they *would* talk to a bounty hunter. Especially if the bail jumper the hunters were looking for was dangerous.

"Valens was wearing a university T-shirt," she added, trying to remember details of the attack yesterday while tamping down the painful feelings that started to creep up when she turned her thoughts in that direction. A sickening fear uncoiled in her stomach, and her imagination started to gallop toward the horrible way that yesterday's abduction could have ended. She or her mom could have been killed. Maybe even both of them.

Lord, I know You are with me, always, she prayed silently. She took a steadying breath, exhaled and turned to Justine. "Your oldest son, Robbie, goes to the university, right? Maybe he's seen Tony Valens around on campus."

Justine turned to her. "Why would you think Robbie would know him?"

Daisy shrugged. "It's possible that Valens never set foot on campus and he just got the shirt because he thought it looked cool. It's also possible that he's an enrolled student. The cops will check on that. But maybe he got the shirt so he'll look like he fits in while hanging out around the student union, or maybe some place off campus, selling drugs. So maybe Robbie's seen him. Would you send him a picture and ask? If he has seen Valens, it would give Martin and me an idea of where to look for him."

Justine nodded. "Okay."

Daisy sent Valens's photo to Justine, then she got up and headed for the coffeepot again. She still didn't have much energy. She wasn't surprised. Over the course of the last two nights, she'd gotten very little sleep. While she was reaching for the handle of the carafe, Millie walked up to her.

"Honey, I'll bet what you really need is something to eat. Why don't you and Martin take an early lunch. I've got a slow cooker full of potato leek soup that should be ready by now. There's shredded cheddar cheese and some crumbled, cooked bacon in the refrigerator for you to sprinkle on top."

That actually sounded really good. "It's your soup," Daisy said. "You and Alvis should eat first."

"I'm not hungry," Alvis said.

Daisy laughed. Alvis was always hungry.

"I will boldly admit that I would like to eat," Martin said. He looked at Daisy and lifted his chin. "Come on, let's go."

Mildly annoyed with herself for giving in to Martin so easily, Daisy walked with him up the stairs to the third floor. After giving Bowie the attention the pup demanded and offering a few scratches to Reggie, who was lying on the top floor of his fancy cat tree, they headed to the kitchen. Daisy was reaching for soup bowls in the cabinet when her phone rang. When she saw the name on the screen, her stomach clenched. She looked at Martin and said, "It's my brother." She took a breath and then answered the call.

"What's going on?" Aaron demanded.

Daisy hesitated, remembering her conversation with her mother. Shannon didn't want Aaron to worry, especially when there was nothing he could do to help in the situation. Daisy felt the same way, but she also didn't feel right deceiving her brother. She told herself she wouldn't lie to him. She'd just avoid telling him the whole truth. For now. Even as she made the decision, it didn't sit well with her. "Things are like usual," she said. "I'm working on throwing a would-be escapee from justice back into jail."

"Knock it off," Aaron snapped. "I know what happened to you and Mom. Gerald thought I knew about it. Sent me a text asking if there's anything he can do to help." Gerald was one of Aaron's old high school buddies. "I haven't talked to Mom, yet," Aaron continued. "I wanted to talk to you first. Are the two of you okay?"

Daisy sighed. "We're both fine."

"Where are you?" he asked. "Are you alone? Can you talk freely?"

"I can talk. I'm at the bail bond office. With Martin."

"With Martin? Put me on speaker."

She tapped the speaker button.

"I'm here," Martin said.

"I thought I could trust you," Aaron said.

Martin's dark eyes widened. Daisy could see the pain in them. "I'm sorry," she said to Martin. "I shouldn't have put you in this position." Then to Aaron, she said, "You're thousands of miles away. Mom and I didn't want you to worry. There's nothing you can do. Nothing we need you to do right now."

"I'll take emergency leave and get there as fast as I can."

"Aaron, *no*." Daisy was still holding her phone. With her free hand, she rubbed her forehead. She could feel a headache coming on. Not because of her brother. She knew he was upset because he loved her and their mom. She was just tired. Of pretty much everything, right now. "Listen to me," she said, struggling to keep her voice sounding confident and calm. Getting into a shouting match with her control freak older brother right now, or bursting into tears, would not help anything.

"Please wait," she said. "For Mom's sake. You have so little time to spend with her. With us. You know how much Mom loves it when you come home and she can show you off to her friends. Have the family over. Go out to dinner, all of us together. Go hiking or fishing together, take a weekend trip over to the coast. If you come now, we won't be able to do any of those things."

Aaron was quiet for a few seconds. "I don't know if I should believe you. Maybe the situation is worse than you're letting on."

Daisy glanced at Martin.

"If it were me, I'd want to know the truth," he said firmly.

"The criminals I'm chasing have targeted me," she said to her brother. "I honestly doubt they'll bother Mom again. She's staying with Aunt Jessica and Uncle Tim. Kidnapping her was a means to get to me. To try to stop me from chasing them."

"I don't like this." Aaron didn't sound happy.

"If we need you to come home, I'll tell you. I promise," she said.

"Martin, you heard that promise, right?"

"I did, Aaron. Call me anytime and I'll give you an update."

Aaron grumbled a little more, which was part of his personality and something he tended to do, anyway.

Finally, he said his goodbyes and disconnected so that he could call their mom.

"Thank you," Daisy said to Martin, thinking about how much stronger she felt when he was with her. And how much she appreciated his opinion—especially in tricky situations like this call with her brother—and his strength of character. The man had a very clear moral compass. And that was a valuable characteristic in anyone.

He gestured for her to sit at the dining table while he got their soup. Watching him take care of things, take care of her, warmed her heart. But it also made it ache at the same time. He would make a good partner in life. A good husband. A good father, even. And yet he lived his life as if he weren't interested in any of those things. And she'd already invested too much time in thinking, hoping, *praying* that things could be different. That he might want something different. Something more. With her.

Knowing that he would head back to Stone River after this case was finished and she wouldn't see him for weeks—months even—she tried to dampen the feelings she had for him. He'd broken her heart a few times already with his determination to be independent. She couldn't keep letting that happen. She needed to create some emotional distance between them.

By the time he set the bowl of soup in front of her, complete with cheese and bacon sprinkled on top, a sense of heavy weariness seemed to have settled over Daisy's entire body. At the moment they didn't have any hot leads on Tony Valens, Beau Daltrey or Ivan Bunker.

Maybe this afternoon would be a good time to go to her apartment and get a little rest.

Tonight, with renewed energy, she could go back to hunting bad guys with a vengeance. It seemed like they were always more active after dark, anyway. And if she wanted to stay alive, she needed to find them, before they found her.

SEVEN

"I realize college students aren't typically known for wanting to wake up early," Daisy said, "but there have to be a few early risers milling around by now. Let's head over to the Dawson campus. It's possible Tony might be there trying to make some quick money selling drugs. And if we don't see him, we can ask around and see if anybody knows him or knows about him." She stepped toward a table and grabbed the stack of mug shot photos she'd printed yesterday. "We'd better take a few of these. Some people might not know him by name, but they'd know him by sight."

Martin, who was sitting in one of the desk chairs in the Peak Bail Bonds office, glanced up at her.

Yesterday after lunch, Daisy had decided to go lie down for a while in her apartment. Five hours later she'd stumbled downstairs to the office, with her hair adorably mussed and cute sleep creases on her face, demanding to know why no one had woken her. Millie had gently reminded her that she hadn't *asked* anyone to wake her up. And even better, Millie had been able to convince her to stay in for the rest of the night and resume her hunt for the perpetrators in the morning.

That had been a huge relief for Martin. Having her out looking for criminals intent on killing her when she was not at full working capacity was a tragedy waiting to happen. But now she was in front of him, impatiently bouncing on her toes, brimming with energy to get hunting. The jerks they were chasing probably underestimated her. Martin never did. He knew the heart and strength of the woman, the drive and the intelligence.

He realized he was staring at her again—this wasn't the first time he'd caught himself doing it—and he made himself turn away. There were limits on what he could offer her, and she deserved so much more. More than Martin could give. Because how could you contribute to a happy, stable marriage when you didn't grow up seeing one? Yeah, he'd observed families that didn't scream and fight and throw things all the time. He'd met Daisy's family before Mr. Lopez was killed and seen the loving relationships between her parents.

But visiting with someone was nowhere near the same as being with them full-time, seeing up close how they dealt with everything, the bad as well as the good. And really, it always came back to the same argument, anyway. Why risk messing things up and possibly losing the best relationship of his life by throwing romance into the mix?

"Okay," he finally said, after taking a few seconds to stand, tuck his phone in his pocket and get his thoughts focused back on the task at hand rather than on his feelings for Daisy. "Let's go."

Steve, who was manning the front counter, as usual,

lifted a hand in a casual goodbye. He'd already taped a sign to the front door letting people know that only one client would be allowed inside the office at a time—no family members or friends allowed with them. They were still open for business, but the door was being kept locked for now.

"I think Steve and I should go out to the university instead of you," Alvis said, heading over to a row of hooks on the wall to reach for his jacket and his battered old slouch hat.

Steve turned in his chair so that he was facing everyone in the back of the office, his eyes wide with excitement and a broad smile plastered on his face. He'd recently expressed an interest in being trained as a bounty hunter.

Daisy turned to Alvis, wearing a guarded expression. "Why?"

"There's a lot of open space on that campus," he answered, shrugging into his jacket. "A shooter could plug you from a long way off. And then get away without being seen."

"I don't—" Daisy started to speak again and Alvis cut her off.

"I know the odds are there isn't an assassin roaming the grounds there just waiting to take a shot at you this morning. And I know you'd keep your eyes open after you left here. You're good at spotting a tail. Good, but not perfect. Steve and I will go." Alvis reached for the photos in Daisy's hand. A lot of bounty hunters went old-school with printed pictures. The last thing they wanted to do was hand their phone over to strangers so they could get a good look at a picture on a screen. Especially given the types of strangers they often talked to.

"I used to have informants at the university," Alvis continued, "but I don't anymore. It's time I got out there and got me some new ones."

Steve was already on his feet. He'd put on his jacket and looked ready to go. Martin watched Millie walk over to take Steve's seat at the counter, smile in response to the excited grin on his face and then pick up a clipboard and take a look at the names of high flight-risk clients scheduled to check in during the day.

"Did you hear anything back from your son?" Martin asked Justine. "Has he ever heard of Tony Valens? Did he recognize his picture?"

Justine leaned back in her chair, crossed her arms and shook her head. "Robbie doesn't know the guy. Doesn't know anything about him."

"Could Robbie meet up with Alvis and Steve?" Daisy asked her. "Maybe help them out. Introduce them to people or show them where students tend to congregate off campus."

"I'll send him a text right now and ask him." Justine glanced at Alvis. "I'll let you know as soon as I hear back from him."

After Alvis and Steve left, Millie asked Daisy, "What do you and Martin plan to do today?"

"Well, we know law enforcement are doing their high-tech research and tracking to find Daltrey and Bunker, as well as Tony Valens," Daisy said slowly, clearly thinking out loud. "Meanwhile, bounty hunters do our best work when we find out our target's habits, or small details about them, and then go out and talk to people. It was the low-tech leads we found, the shopping bag and the pizza box at the rental house, that got us to the part of town where they had that industrial space off the alley and were hiding my mom."

"So, you're saying you want to go back to that part of town?" Martin asked.

"I am. I've tried calling Louis at QuickStop several times and he won't pick up. Same with Janis at the hair salon. So the idea that those informants didn't want to talk to me in plain sight of anybody, but that they might talk to me on the phone instead, didn't pan out.

"Something happened in that part of town that spooked people," she added. "I want to talk to the tenants in the buildings around that abandoned building where Valens stashed Mom and me. I have no idea where to even look for Daltrey and Bunker at the moment. That makes Tony Valens the best lead we have. And we know from the cops that he frequents the old part of downtown. Somebody has to have seen him around there. Seen *something* that would be helpful to us. If we get enough small bits of information, maybe we could piece together a bigger picture."

"That sounds like a good plan to me," Millie said. And then she pointed to a figure standing at the front door.

"Detective Gerber," Martin said, walking past Daisy to open the door for him.

After a quick greeting, the detective cut to the chase. "I came by to let you know that we found Tony Valens."

Daisy's face lit up. "Have you gotten any good information out of him?"

Gerber sighed. "I'm afraid not. He's dead."

Martin felt his stomach drop with disappointment, while he kept his eyes on Daisy. He watched her smile settle into a more somber expression. And then saw her lift her chin. He could almost see her strengthening her resolve. It reminded him of the months after her father was killed, when she was determined to help bring the hit-and-run driver to justice. And just like back then, his heart filled with admiration for her.

"What happened to him?" Daisy asked.

"He was murdered. Shot execution style."

"Just like an organized crime hit man would do it," Martin said. "You figure the killer was Daltrey or Bunker?"

"We're determined to consider all possibilities until the facts are in," Gerber said. "The crime techs are processing the scene right now. But yeah, we strongly suspect Daltrey or Bunker were involved. Or both of them."

"This whole situation is spinning out of control very quickly," Millie said quietly while looking at Daisy.

The detective nodded. "I wanted to keep you in the loop. Be careful."

He left, and Millie picked up her phone. "I'll text Alvis and let him know that he and Steve can come back to the office."

Daisy turned to Martin, her stubborn, determined chin still lifted. "We've got to get out on the streets and find Daltrey and Bunker before they murder anyone else."

That was exactly what Martin thought she would say. He was proud of her. But he was also a little bit scared for her, too.

"Hey! Louis! Don't run from me, I need to talk to you!" The second Daisy had walked up to the Quick-

Stop door, she'd locked eyes with Louis through the glass. And as soon as she pushed through the door, he'd scurried toward a passage from the main floor of the store to his back office, where there was also an exit out of the building. He was trying to get away without talking to her. And Daisy was having none of that.

"What are you doing?" she demanded, going after him. Louis may know the layout of his store better than her, but Daisy was younger and more limber, and she managed to hop a counter and get in front of him before he could escape.

"I've got nothing to say to you." Louis stubbornly set his jaw and shook his head while the two clerks at the register watched, goggle-eyed.

Daisy heard Martin behind her. He'd walked in for only a few steps and then he'd stopped in a position where he'd have a wider view of the whole store. He'd have a good view of everything going on, including any people who might be in there shopping.

"Look, I just want to ask you a few questions," Daisy said to Louis, holding up her hands in a placating gesture. Now that she had him cornered and he'd stopped trying to flee from her, she took a couple of steps back to give him some space and tried to cool down a bit. The man did not have to talk to her if he didn't want to. She wasn't a cop. He could call the actual cops and have her tossed out. So, much as she wanted to push him to quit playing around and talk to her, she needed to calm things down.

"I'm not getting myself killed for you," Louis said. "I know we've helped each other out over the years, but I've got a family. I've got—"

"Tony Valens is dead," Daisy interrupted. She reached into her pocket and pulled out one of the photos of Valens she'd printed. She unfolded the paper and held the image in front of Louis. "You know him, right?" she said. "You've seen him around?"

Louis nodded wordlessly.

Finally, she was getting somewhere. She exhaled a sigh and relaxed her stance. "I need you to help me find the people who killed him. So let's start from the beginning. Where did you first see him?"

Louis crossed his arms over his chest. Daisy could see that he was biting down on his lips. Something people often did when they were afraid they would blurt out something.

"Valens can't hurt you," she said, struggling to keep the tone of impatience out of her voice. "You can tell me the truth."

"I'm not taking a chance. I don't want the people who killed Valens coming after me."

"Why would they do that?" Daisy could see from his wide eyes and pale skin that he was truly afraid. "They don't even know who you are. Look, the killers had a problem specifically with Valens. That's why they went after him. And they have one with me, too. So I really need your help. Please."

"They know who I am," Louis said, breaking eye contact with her and looking down at the ground.

"You *know* who killed Valens? How is that possible?"

Daisy heard Martin move up closer behind her.

"I started seeing Tony Valens around here about a year ago. Hanging around, meeting up with people for a few minutes before they'd quickly walk or drive away. I figured he might be selling drugs in the neighborhood, but I didn't know for sure. I'm not a cop. It's not my job to know that stuff."

His gaze flicked up to meet Daisy's for a few seconds, then he looked down again. "I saw him with a couple of guys who didn't look or sound like they were from around here. I'd see them in here, or sometimes out walking on the sidewalk together. I didn't think much about it. But then a day before you showed up asking questions about your two bail jumpers, Tony came by and told me to keep my mouth shut if anybody—bounty hunters, cops, whoever—came by asking about him or his friends. Told me if I didn't stay quiet, that some mob people would come after me and make sure I stayed quiet forever."

When she was here before, Louis wouldn't even look at the photos she had of Daltrey and Bunker. Because he'd been terrified. She knew that now. She didn't have any paper photos of the two hit men with her now, so she found the photos on her phone and then held it up to Louis. "Are these the men you saw?" she asked, showing Daltrey and then swiping the screen to show Bunker.

Louis didn't answer. Which, in a way, was an answer.

Daisy would alert Detective Gerber to check out the store, get any video footage they could, check sales transactions and see if either of the hit men left a trail of any kind of useful digital information.

"The cops might come by here later," Daisy said.

Louis's shoulders slumped.

"But I am not telling anyone that you, personally, helped me in any way." She would leave it up to him to decide what he wanted to say to the police. "Is there *anything* you can tell me that might help me find Daltrey and Bunker? Something you noticed about either of them? Something they said to you or that you overheard them saying to one another? Did you notice what they were driving? Any scrap of information could help."

"They came in for cigarettes, mostly. Sometimes beer or food. And gallon-sized jugs of bottled water. That's all I can tell you. It's not like they hung out in here."

Bottled water. Probably because they were staying in that abandoned building with no utilities.

"Thank you," she said, reaching into her pocket for the money she'd tucked in there before she got out of her SUV, and handing it to him. She hadn't learned anything that could help her find the fugitives, but maybe law enforcement would be able to glean something when they came here later. As always, small bits of seemingly random facts could eventually coalesce into useful, actionable information.

"If you really want to thank me," Louis said, "don't come back here for a while." He glanced toward the clerks, who weren't close enough to hear their conversation but were still watching them intently. "And don't try to grill any of my clerks for information. They don't deserve to be put in danger."

That would be something else for the police to deal with.

"Okay." Daisy turned to Martin. "Let's go."

"Wait, I have a question," Martin said to Louis.

A stubborn expression settled on the store owner's face. "I don't know you."

"I realize that," Martin said easily, and then he flashed a smile that had Daisy transfixed. Martin had such sharp features that he tended to look severe much of the time. But then when he flashed those pearly whites, the gentle, playful Martin came through clearly. And Daisy loved seeing that.

She realized where her thoughts were going and she was annoyed. Annoyed with herself, and annoyed with Martin. This was not the time or place to let her thoughts turn in that direction, to consider how charming Martin could be. What was *wrong* with her?

"Ask Louis your question," she snapped.

Martin's smile grew broader. Great. What a time for him to be able to guess her thoughts.

"I was just wondering how Tony Valens and his criminal buddies would know that you had a connection to Daisy," Martin said to Louis. "I don't imagine you go around telling people that you work with a bounty hunter."

Louis shook his head. "How would I know?" He looked at Daisy. "You and I talk in here and sometimes outside in the parking lot in broad daylight. I don't tell people I help a bounty hunter. But it's not like we hide, either. I just figured they must have seen us together."

With a huff of impatience, Louis stalked off toward his office and out of sight. The interview was officially over.

"What do you want to do next?" Martin asked Daisy as they walked out the door.

Daisy needed a few minutes to consider that. The problem was, she couldn't afford to waste any time.

Daltrey and Bunker were planning to skip town

eventually. She had no doubt about that. They'd already murdered Jimmy Nestor, who'd shown them the rec center at the lake where they'd tried to set their trap for Daisy. Now they'd killed Tony Valens. They apparently liked to tie up loose ends as they lived their criminal lives. And Daisy was one of those loose ends. They weren't planning to let her live.

"Welcome to our home," Jessica Cassidy said to Martin after she gave her niece, Daisy, a lingering hug at the threshold of the front door. "It's been a long time since you were last here."

"Yes, ma'am, it has." Martin accepted the welcoming hug she offered him and then stepped inside and shook hands with her husband, Tim.

Jessica was Shannon Lopez's older sister. Martin had been to the house, on the edge of a fifty-acre parcel of land with a stocked pond in the center of it, a few times back when he and Daisy and Aaron had all been in high school together.

He'd also been there, helping out however he could, after the funeral services for Daisy's father. Jessica and Tim had hosted an open house for everyone who wanted to come by and visit with the family. Martin had stayed out of the way, cooking, cleaning, doing his best to entertain bored, cranky kids who had no way of understanding the gravity of the situation. He hadn't needed to visit with the family because he'd been with them since he'd learned of Mr. Lopez's fatal accident. As soon as he got the call, he'd blasted over from Stone River and ended up staying for about three weeks.

"Hey, how are you kids holding up?" Shannon met them in the living room.

Like Daisy, she had dark circles under her eyes and some bruising on her face. Heartbreak, anger and determination formed a knot in Martin's throat. He took a couple of deep breaths, pushed the grim emotions aside and did his best to smile when she looked in his direction.

Jessica and Tim hung around to chat for a few minutes. Then, after Daisy and Martin politely turned down their offer to make some coffee, they left the room. "We'll let you talk privately," Jessica said before they headed toward the den at the other end of the house. "If you get hungry, help yourselves to anything in the kitchen."

Shannon dropped down onto the sofa and Daisy sat close beside her, reaching for her mom's hand and squeezing it.

This had been Daisy's idea, coming here late in the afternoon to talk to her mom. She wanted to ask her some questions and maybe get some leads, depending on the answers. She told Martin that she'd thought about doing it ever since she was released from the hospital, but she wanted to give her mom time to rest and recover a bit.

"I'm sorry to have to make you go through all of this again," Daisy said to her mom, "thinking about what happened from the time you were kidnapped to the end of it all. But since I was getting checked out at the hospital while you were being questioned by the police, and Martin was wasting his time hanging around with me instead of working on the case and listening in on your statement to the police, I don't know a lot of the details about what happened to you."

Daisy glanced at Martin with a serious expression on her face, but also a teasing glint in her eye.

Yeah, tough girl, you can give me a hard time about hanging around the hospital with you if you want, Martin thought. *But you were glad I was there.*

And he was glad, and grateful, that he was there, too.

"I was outside, about to get into my car and go to the grocery store, when those two mobsters grabbed me," Shannon said, her voice quavering a little.

She went on to describe how she was taken at gunpoint. That Jimmy Nestor was already in the SUV the fugitives were using. How they took her to the rec center, tied her up and made the recording to send to Daisy.

After the shoot-out at the shopping mall, they drove to the forest on the west side of town near Pearce Park and waited until dark. Then they took her to the abandoned building downtown where they locked her up in a windowless office. She'd seen Tony Valens for a few brief moments before she was locked up.

"I thought they were going to leave me in that office to die," Shannon said, letting go of Daisy's hand to wrap her arms around herself as if she felt a chill.

Daisy leaned against her mom's shoulder. "I'm sorry." Her voice caught in her throat. It sounded like she was fighting back tears. "It's my fault this happened to you."

"No." Shannon shook her head emphatically. "These people decided to do evil things. That decision is on them." She turned to Daisy. "You do everything you can to bring people who hurt others to justice, and I am so proud of you for that."

She turned to Martin. "And I am so proud of you, too."

Martin felt his eyes sting a little. Neither of his parents had ever told him that they were proud of him. And he'd convinced himself that wasn't a big deal. Until now. The truth was, having someone say those words to him felt good.

"I was certain they weren't going to let me live, because they didn't hesitate to kill that man at the rec center." Shannon closed her eyes for a few seconds and took a couple of deep breaths. "And also because they spoke so freely in front of me, to each other and on phone calls, it was pretty clear they weren't worried about what I might tell the police." She shook her head. "They weren't planning on me being alive to tell the authorities anything."

"What did they talk about in front of you?" Martin asked.

"The main thing I remember is what I told the police sergeant when Daisy and I were first rescued. That their mob boss wasn't too happy with them nearly being captured by a bounty hunter in Montana. That they needed to tie up loose ends so they sent a message about how dangerous their organization was and they didn't give the impression they were a bunch of weak idiots. That they had to kill Daisy." Shannon sniffed loudly.

"From what I could hear, they weren't given permission to jump bail back in Miami," she added. "The mob bosses wanted them to keep their mouths shut, go to trial and do prison time if they had to. But they didn't want to do that. So they ran, heading first to Atlanta, and then here. I overheard other things about mob stuff, but I don't remember much of the details. It's kind of a blur." She turned to Daisy. "But I heard the boss say that they had to kill you if they wanted to get back into his good graces. That they couldn't afford to let their competitors—or the cops—see a small-town bounty hunter get the best of them."

Daisy turned to Martin. "So what exactly do you think we're dealing with? Are their mob cronies here in Jameson helping them to find me and kill me, or are they doing it all on their own?"

"I don't know." Martin held her gaze as several possible scenarios of what could happen if they didn't find Daltrey and Bunker in time—all of them terrifying—played through his mind. "I don't know. I do know we have *got* to find where Daltrey and Bunker are hiding. The question is, where do we start?"

"Start with what you know," Daisy said softly, repeating her favorite bounty hunting advice. "Daltrey and Bunker drove out to Pearce Park when they had Mom. And that's where their truck was found abandoned. Maybe they feel safe there. Maybe they've gone back there. Or maybe some long-term camper out there saw something. Like the vehicle Daltrey and Bunker drove away in after they abandoned the truck."

That was a lot of *maybes*. What Martin wanted was definite answers. Two mob hit men were coming after Daisy to kill her. It was possible they had additional help. The bad guys needed to be captured, *now*.

Martin's biggest fear—besides the possibility of Daisy getting killed—was that Daltrey and Bunker would find a good place to lie low for a while, until the heat was off and law enforcement turned their attention toward other, newer, seemingly more pressing crimes. And then the assassins would come after Daisy.

Please guide us, Lord, Martin prayed silently.

And then, to Daisy, he said, "Okay. Tomorrow morning, after the sun comes up and we can see what we're doing. Let's go out to Pearce Park and see if we can find any sign of them."

EIGHT

"If we wait until the sun is completely up, Daltrey and Bunker might see us coming if they're here in the park," Daisy said.

"True," Martin responded. "But if we go in when it's too dark, we could stumble over them before we know they're there."

"Okay." She looked toward the ridgeline to the east of them, where the skyline was already turning a lighter shade of blue. "We'll wait a couple more minutes."

They were in Martin's truck, parked on the northern edge of the sprawling Pearce Park Campground parking lot. There was no campground attendant on-site this late in the season, but people were still allowed to camp in the park until the first heavy snowfall. After that, the access roads would be closed up and the pipes carrying fresh water to the campground would be closed off and drained so they didn't freeze and rupture in the winter.

If Martin were on his own, he would already be searching for the fugitives in the darkness. He'd done it plenty of times in the past, successfully finding the target he was tracking. He could move silently through the forest. Daisy, on the other hand, was not so quiet. She was a good tracker in the woods. Her dad had taught her some very useful skills. She was mindful of her movements, and disciplined. To a point. And then her impatience kicked in. At which point she would step on a stick or kick a rock, make some kind of sound that would alert a forest creature that would then chirp or scurry away in alarm and then their cover would be blown.

He'd tried talking to her about it, but it didn't help. Nobody could be good at everything. And in Daisy's case, any time she fell short of her aspirations she tended to beat herself up pretty hard. Especially when it came to bounty hunting. She focused on the searches so intently, wanting so badly to see that justice was served, that any stumble or shortcoming on her part became a personal failure in her mind.

Martin had told her to lighten up about it once, and had nearly gotten an iced tea flung in his face for his troubles. So he kept his mouth shut. For now. But he would probably approach the topic again at some point when things weren't so tense.

"Since the cops came out here and did an area search after the abandoned truck was discovered, didn't find Daltrey or Bunker, and left, I think there's a fair chance our fugitives came back," Daisy said. "They can't rent a motel room without running the risk of having the cops alerted. This place is familiar to them. And if they stayed out here, they wouldn't exactly be in plain sight."

"It's about time to get out of the truck and hit the ground," Martin said. "What do you want to do?"

"Head into the forest about fifty or a hundred yards

until we connect with one of the paths crisscrossing the campground and see what we can find. I can't imagine our fugitives hiking deep into the forest, packing food, water and weapons and a tent or sleeping bag. It's not like they're looking to stay for a long time and set up residence. They just want to hang around Jameson long enough to kill me, get back into favor with their criminal friends and then have those friends help them get out of town before anyone can find them."

"All right. And depending on the situation, we might want to question any campers we come across and find out if they've seen anything helpful," Martin said.

The top edge of the sun finally crested the mountain peaks to the east, sending gold rays of sunlight streaming through the branches of the surrounding towering pines. Martin could now clearly see the fear and uncertainty visible in Daisy's eyes despite the confident tone of her voice. If she were looking closely at him, she would probably see the fear in his eyes, as well. Fear that he might lose her. Because the truth was the good guys didn't always win. Not in this lifetime.

He held out his hand toward her. And after a slight hesitation, she slipped her hand into his. "Lord, please protect us and everyone else connected to this search," he prayed. "Please help us find the men we're looking for. And help us to remember that You are with us always. Amen."

"Amen," Daisy echoed, squeezing his hand before she let go. "Let's get to work."

They got out of the truck, both of them carrying sidearms tucked into holsters. But they'd agreed that they wanted to avoid firing shots if at all possible. There were people here in the park, and a bullet flying through the air could easily pass through the thick pine needles and hit an innocent unseen person.

Daisy led the way to a path in the woods not far from the parking lot. "This leads to a cluster of campsites with dug-in grills that make it easy to start a fire and keep it going. Maybe they'll be camped there. It's below freezing at night now. Our fugitives will need to stay warm. Plus, there's a spigot where campers can get fresh, clean water. That could draw them, too."

They followed the path, and soon Martin smelled something cooking. After a couple of sniffs, he decided it was bacon. The path turned and thin smoke drifted into view.

"Let's slow down," Daisy said. "Try to look like we're campers out for a morning walk instead of bounty hunters searching for somebody."

"If we see them but they don't see us, let's just keep walking," Martin suggested. "We can call the cops, get enough people out here to set up a secure perimeter and then capture them."

"Agreed," Daisy said. "I'm way beyond caring about who makes the arrest or about me earning the bounty recovery fee. I just want them locked up."

Most of the campsites were empty. The rising sun warmed the light layer of frost that had formed on the pine needles, creating droplets that fell whenever Martin or Daisy brushed against them.

They moved closer to the inhabited site that was the source of the smoke and scent of bacon cooking.

Through the tree branches alongside the trail, Martin
spotted two men by the cookfire, with two small tents
behind them. He moved his hand toward his gun, despite his intention not to use it in a setting where there
could be innocent civilians potentially in his line of
fire. But sometimes a situation arose when you didn't
have much of a choice and you had to do something you
didn't really want to. If the men at the campsite turned
out to be Daltrey and Bunker, and they came out shooting, Martin would have to respond in kind.

He glanced at Daisy. She'd slowed her walk considerably as she tried to get a good look. The men were
wearing hoodies pulled up and cinched, heads tilted
down toward the bacon sizzling in frying pans, faces
not clearly visible. Their hands were tucked in their
pockets, where they could be holding guns.

A crow cawed loudly from a pine branch behind the
bounty hunters. Martin immediately spun around, his
heart hammering in his chest. The shadowy creature
flapped its wings and flew off, leaving bouncing green
branches and a cascade of falling droplets in its wake.

Were they being followed? Should he and Daisy take
cover? As a bounty hunter, Martin had to strike a balance between caution and taking action. That wasn't
always easy to do. Especially when someone he cared
about was targeted for murder.

As they drew closer to the men by the cookfire, Martin quickly considered what he would do if he were in
Daltrey's or Bunker's shoes. He would probably separate
from his partner while they were at the campground.
People who were hunting the fugitives would be looking

for *two* men together. Plus, it would be smart to have one man keep watch some distance away from their camping spot while the other one slept. And there was no arguing against the reality that these hit men were smart.

So he and Daisy didn't just need to get a closer look any time they saw two guys together out here. They needed to check out individuals, too. And hope that they hadn't already been spotted by one or both of the fugitives the minute they drove into the parking lot. And all of that was on the assumption the men were here. They might not be.

They were finally just about even with the two men at the cooking fire. "Get ready," Daisy whispered. "I've got to make some kind of noise so they'll look at me and I can see their faces."

Not exactly what Martin wanted to hear. But it was a reasonable action. If they weren't assertive in their search, they were wasting their time.

Before they were in full view of the men, Daisy kicked a rock. It skittered across the path, hit a tree trunk and made enough noise for the men to look up. And then one of them looked back at the cast-iron skillet over the fire and called out, "Food's just about ready!"

A woman crawled out from one of the tents. A second woman emerged from the other one.

The men were not Daltrey and Bunker.

Martin and Daisy continued along the trail for a while, passing only one other campsite that was inhabited. A man and woman looked like they'd set up permanent housing, with a tent big enough to hold a large family. The couple were friendly and waved to Martin and Daisy.

"We're looking for a couple of people," Daisy said after their initial greeting. She showed them pictures of Daltrey and Bunker.

"These are the guys the cops were out here looking for," the man said. The woman nodded vigorously in agreement. "These two left a truck up here, I think. The cops towed it away after they came through the campground questioning everybody. We never saw those two men ourselves. Heard they were wanted for some kind of crimes."

"So you haven't seen the two men in these pictures around here?" Daisy asked. "Are you sure? Because they might have come back to this area in the last couple of days."

The man and woman looked at each other, shook their heads and then turned back to Daisy. "No," the woman said. "Haven't seen them."

After talking to the couple, Martin and Daisy headed back toward his truck. Their hike around the campgrounds didn't get them the result they wanted—they hadn't found any sign of Daltrey and Bunker—but that was part of bounty hunting. Sometimes you put energy into something and didn't get a payoff.

At least Daltrey and Bunker hadn't launched an attack on them from the cover of the forest. That was something. Knowing the hit men had spent time right here in the park and specifically this campground still gave Martin an edgy feeling, even if the assassins weren't here right now.

Daisy sighed heavily as they walked. "Well, there's a whole lot of park that we haven't covered yet and we can't check it all. We might as well head back to the office and see if we can drum up some other leads to follow."

They made their way out of the forest to the edge of the parking lot, then walked through the dappled sunlight to Martin's truck parked beneath a tall pine.

When they got closer to the truck, Martin looked down and his blood ran cold.

All four of the truck's tires were slashed.

"It might have been vandals with nothing better to do," Daisy said, doing a quick turn completely around after noticing the ruined tires to see if she needed to be *really* worried. She didn't see anybody watching them. "Maybe it was just bored kids."

"You don't really believe that," Martin said.

"I want to."

Her hand shook with adrenaline as she pulled her phone out of her pocket. "I've got a good mechanic," she said. "He'll dispatch a tow truck right away. Peak Bail Bonds will pay for the damage."

"I'm not worried about that," Martin said tightly.

Daisy tapped her screen a couple of times, listened to the call connect and start to ring at the other end, and then heard the crack of gunshots and the dull *thunk* of bullets hitting Martin's truck right beside her.

"Gun!" Martin yelled, and they sprinted side by side across the parking lot, away from the shooter and into the woods.

Daisy fought to keep her footing while running on uneven ground and rocks for several yards. Finally, she took a quick glance at Martin running beside her. "Did you see the shooter?" she gasped, her lungs already burning from exertion and tight with fear.

"No." They were moving into a stretch of downward-sloping terrain that would eventually take them to one of the many tributaries of the Spruce River.

"We need to head to the base of the cliffs by the river," Daisy called over to Martin. "If we get down there we can find a place where our backs are covered and we can see anyone who's coming after us."

"Good idea," he replied.

Daisy had fished down there with her brother and her parents many times as a kid.

She reached for her phone to call for help and felt sickened when she realized she didn't have it. She must have dropped it when the gunshots startled her in the parking lot. Or else she'd tucked it into her pocket out of habit and it fell out when she'd started running.

"Phone," she called out. They had to call for help. They were in the Montana wilderness. If someone had heard the shots fired at Martin and Daisy in the parking lot, they might not realize that it meant someone was in danger. They might think somebody was just target practicing and not bother to report it.

Martin looked in her direction and she saw him reach into his pocket. The next thing she knew, he grabbed her arm, yanking her with him as he took cover behind a pair of trees with thick trunks that had grown close enough together to form a useful barricade.

They crouched down together and she watched him dial 9-1-1. He turned the volume low on his phone, and when the dispatcher answered he explained what had happened, described their current location and told her where they were headed. While he was doing that, Daisy listened intently for sounds that anyone had tracked them this far.

She heard something, like dirt and rocks moving downslope toward them. She reached over to touch Martin and get his attention. He immediately stopped talking and tapped a button to silence his phone.

Leaden fear settled in the pit of Daisy's stomach as she tried to determine if the sound came from someone who was tracking them or if it was just the movement of ground she and Martin had disturbed themselves while they were running. The sounds grew louder and it sounded like the unsettled earth sliding toward them was moving faster.

Panic could lead to bad decisions and create significant danger in a life-and-death situation, so before they started blindly running again, Daisy wanted to get a better assessment of their situation. For all she knew, the small rockslide could be part of a trap meant to send her and Martin running directly toward someone armed and waiting to finish them off.

She gestured at Martin, indicating that she wanted to peek around their tree barricade and take a look in the direction they'd just come from and see if anyone was there.

Martin nodded and pulled his pistol from his holster and held it near his face, ready to sight any potential target. "I'll cover you," he said, moving so that he was behind her and slightly to her right.

"Stay behind me and look over my shoulder," she said.

From that position, if anyone took a shot at her, Martin would see it and be ready to shoot back.

"Got it," he said.

"All right," she said, *"now."*

She leaned around the tree trunk and felt her heart fall to her feet when she realized Martin had ignored her directions and stepped out into the open, effectively drawing fire to himself while she stayed almost completely protected behind the tree.

The sound of gunshots rent the air. A single long gun by the sound of it. A rifle, its bullets hitting with frightening accuracy as they struck the side of the tree, eye level with Daisy, before she'd even been able to discern any human figure in the shadowy forest. She dived back behind the tree and heard more bullets hitting the trunk and the ground.

Martin returned fire, though he had only a handgun and the rifle sounded like it was some distance away, so it wasn't very likely that he'd hit his target. But his shooting stopped the rifle fire, for the moment.

When he dived to the ground behind Daisy, she turned and saw a swath of blood blooming red across the left side of his face.

"You're hurt!" She crawled toward him but he wiped his forearm across his cheek before she could reach him. When she got closer, she could see three jagged cuts on his face. They were small, but they looked deep.

"It's nothing. A bullet hit something that broke apart and flew at me. A rock or tree bark, maybe. Could have been a pine cone." He wiped his face again with his sleeve and gave her a half smile. "I'm still handsome, right?"

She didn't want to laugh. She wanted to be mad. But this was Martin; this was simply how he was. And he had a strong hold on her heart.

"I don't know how the shooter missed taking your head completely off with you just walking out into the open like that." Daisy was fighting back tears of fear and frustration because she knew that Martin had intentionally put himself in danger to protect her. "Do you not know how to follow directions?"

He looked at her, his eyes appearing a little darker than usual. "Sometimes it's a challenge."

She sighed deeply and shook her head. "We need to start moving again."

"If whoever is shooting at us has any brains at all, it's got to be obvious to them that we're heading toward the river," Martin said. "We've got to change plans. Maybe head east and then circle back closer to the parking lot. The cops should be there any minute. We've just got to stay alive until they show up."

Daisy heard a voice in the direction the rifle shots had come from. And it sounded familiar. Daltrey or Bunker, she wasn't sure which one. Was he talking to a second person who was there in the forest, or was he talking on the phone? She couldn't tell. Was he coordinating his position with someone else? Getting ready to surround her and Martin?

The voice sounded close and it was getting closer. The person was walking toward them.

Martin stood, reached for Daisy's hand and pulled her to her feet. "We've got to go, *now.*"

As soon as they started to move, shots rang out. Fear sent Daisy's heart leaping up into her throat. She didn't dare look back. That could slow her down. She nearly lost her balance a couple of times as she ran over rocks and pine cones and tree roots, but she kept moving. Martin was faster and surer-footed than she was in the forest, she knew that, but he stayed by her side instead of running ahead.

To her left she heard the voice call out again—she still couldn't tell whether it was Daltrey or Bunker—and she turned to see which one it was. Not looking where she was going, she ran too close to the edge of a ravine. Her body fell through the air for the span of a couple of heartbeats, landing with a hard thump that knocked the air out of her and then beginning its spiral downward. The soft, loamy soil slid with her as she rolled and tumbled through tall yellowed wild grass and prickly bushes and shrubs, finally coming to a stop against the base of a tree.

Her head was still spinning when she pushed herself to a seated position. She knew she was in danger, but at first all she could do was just sit there.

And then she heard a laugh. Not a teasing, light-hearted, Martin-type laugh. But a darker, ill-willed one, filled with malice.

Her eyes finally focused on the figure of a man standing in the shadows under the trees. It took Daisy a moment to realize who was in front of her. It was Ivan Bunker, but he looked different. His mustache was gone and his reddish hair had been dyed blond.

He had something in his hand. Given the shape of it, she assumed it was a rifle. He must have been the person shooting at her and Martin a couple of minutes ago.

"I can't believe you ended up coming right to me,"

he said, shaking his head. "So much for the hotshot bounty hunter. You really are dumb."

Daisy tried to get to her feet, but Bunker moved quickly. Before she could stand, he backhanded her across the face, sending her chin snapping toward her shoulder and throwing her off balance. Before she could right herself, he'd snatched away her gun.

She drew in a ragged breath, but she couldn't quite lift her head. Couldn't get her thoughts together other than to whisper a short prayer. "Dear Lord, help me."

Bunker laughed again. This time it was an icy-cold chuckle. "Oh, if I only had a dollar for every time I've heard that right before I pulled the trigger, I'd be a rich man."

How many times had this creep terrorized someone? How many times had his been the last face someone saw before their life was over? Bunker and Daltrey had been charged with two counts of murder in Miami. They'd killed Jimmy Nestor and presumably Tony Valens, too. The hit man in front of her wouldn't hesitate to add a bounty hunter to the list.

She heard her own harsh breathing, made uneven by her physical pain and her fear. Then she heard another sound. Something that didn't sound natural in the forest.

Car engines. The strangely robotic sound of voices being carried over radio transmissions. The police. Martin's plan must have worked. During their final sprint before she'd fallen, they'd made their way back closer to the parking lot.

"If you shoot me, those cops will hear it and they'll find you," Daisy said without looking up. Despite her usual bravado, the truth was, if she was going to get shot, she didn't really want to see it coming.

"No, they won't," Bunker said. "I'll barely make a sound. They won't know what happened until they find you dead."

Her head felt heavy, but she forced herself to lift it so she could look at him. Slowly, she focused on the long object he held in his hand. He wasn't carrying a rifle, after all. Instead, he held a hunting bow.

"Daltrey's got the rifle," Bunker said. "Me, I came to Montana because I wanted to do some sport hunting." He glanced at his bow as he lifted it to his shoulder. "These things are great. And you don't attract attention the same way you do when you buy a gun."

Daisy somehow managed to shove herself to her feet and started shakily backing away.

"Go ahead," he said. "Waste your energy running if you want to. That will make it more fun for me. And even if you yell, even if the cops do hear you—which I doubt will happen—it won't matter. I've got steel-tipped arrows. Lots of them. You'll bleed out before help arrives."

Daisy wrenched her body around and started to run, her training kicking in as she remembered to move in a zigzag pattern. But in the end, that didn't help. She heard a twanging sound, and then felt a searing pain in her upper right arm that sent her spinning. She stumbled and fell, her forehead smacking hard on the ground.

She opened her eyes. Saw Bunker over her and

notching another arrow. And then she heard the crack of gunfire.

Daltrey, with his rifle, had arrived to join forces with his partner.

NINE

When Martin finally spotted Daisy it took every bit of self-discipline he had to not immediately run straight toward her. It had already taken much of his self-control not to call out her name as he searched for her after she'd stumbled into the ravine, but he hadn't wanted to make it easy for the person tracking them with the rifle to find her if she answered his call.

Now Martin was standing partially hidden by a tree trunk, horrified to see Daisy crouched on the ground with a *hunting arrow* sticking out of her arm.

He stared at the stranger who had an arrow notched in a bow. He was not yet pointing it anywhere other than at the ground. The moment the blond man raised the bow and pointed the arrow at Daisy, Martin would fire a couple of rounds and drop him. But Martin was hesitating for the moment, not wanting to alert the rifle shooter to his location. With Daisy lying there out of commission, so vulnerable, he didn't want to have to deal with two assailants at once. At least two. Maybe there were more.

Daisy's hunch must have been right. Daltrey and

Bunker must have been hiding somewhere around here. And somehow they'd been alerted to Daisy's presence.

The man with the bow stepped forward into the sunlight, closer to Daisy. Now Martin could see that it was Ivan Bunker, that he'd changed his appearance. Daltrey had probably done so, too. And Daltrey was likely the shooter with the rifle. Maybe he was nearby, watching and waiting for Martin to reveal himself as he tried to rescue Daisy so he could finish off the two of them at once.

As he'd intended to do, Martin had led himself and Daisy back closer to the parking lot. It was still some distance away, but in the quiet of the forest sound carried, and he could hear the movement of cars, voices on radios. Moments ago he'd heard the sounds of arriving sirens.

Martin's hand itched to reach for his phone, to call the cops and get them over here to help. But he was afraid to look away from the scene in front of him for even a second. And from the distance where he now stood, he needed both hands on his pistol for sure aim so the bullets would hit their target.

He held his breath and listened for any sound of the rifleman possibly hiding nearby. He didn't hear anything.

But then Bunker—who was either talking to himself or talking to Daisy, it was hard to tell—looked up, shook his head and laughed. Then he pulled back on the bow and aimed the arrow at Daisy, all while stepping closer toward her. Plenty of things could end a life besides a gun. If an arrow hit a vital organ while they were out here in the wilderness, Daisy could be dead before they were anywhere near a hospital.

Martin had no choice. He stood clear of the tree trunk, stepped forward and took the shots. But his movement away from the tree caught Bunker's attention. Bunker saw or heard something. Whatever it was, it was enough warning for the hit man to drop to the ground and let the bullets strike the dirt beside him.

Martin had moved into a clearing to shoot, and now he was committed to taking more aggressive action. He had no choice other than to keep moving through the open space and bring down Bunker. The cops would have heard gunfire by now, but it would take them a few minutes to get oriented and figure out where the shots were coming from. And Martin could not afford to waste that time, not when Daisy was still in danger.

Crouched down and moving quickly, he'd covered about a third of the distance between himself and Bunker when the assassin threw aside the bow and pulled out a handgun, now returning fire at Martin.

Daisy was on the ground between the two men. She moved around on her hands and knees, favoring the injured arm and trying to get to her feet but not quite able to do it. She was looking in every direction, clearly bewildered and apparently unarmed.

Martin kept moving forward, firing again at Bunker, hitting him in the shoulder. The killer spun halfway around, tripping over something and nearly falling, before taking several stumbling steps into a cluster of nearby trees.

Martin heard a rifle shot behind him and saw a puff of dirt by his boot where the bullet struck the ground.

He dropped to his knees and crawled through the yellowing, late-season wild grasses toward Daisy, terrified at the thought that he might get himself killed and leave her alone and unprotected.

The rifleman behind him fired at him again. The bullet nicked the heel of his boot before smacking into the dirt. Bunker, who was in front of him, began shooting at him from his hiding spot under the trees. Martin kept moving toward Daisy.

"Martin?" Daisy called out uncertainly as he moved almost within reach. There were marks on her face that would turn to bruises soon. Grass and leaves and pine straw in her hair. That tumble down the ravine had taken a lot out of her.

"Yeah, it's me," he said, finally crawling up to her and then positioning his body as best he could to protect her from any flying bullets.

She reached for his free hand and gripped it tightly. "Bunker took my gun," she said.

"It's okay." Martin forced a calm smile on his face when what he wanted to do was roar in frustration at all the violence and evil and injustice in the world. And at the same time he wanted to give in to heartbroken tears at seeing Daisy once again injured and in pain. This was too much. All that had happened to her in such a short amount of time was too much.

He wanted to keep holding her hand, but Martin made himself release his grip and reached for his phone to call 9-1-1. "We're being fired at about a mile northeast of the parking lot at Pearce Park," he said as soon as the operator answered, certain she would be aware of the situation. "There are two shooters."

"We are relaying your location to law enforcement on scene," the operator answered back. "Stay on the line."

Martin heard the sound of Ivan Bunker shooting again at him. He didn't dare return fire for fear of hitting one of the cops coming to help.

It seemed like it took forever, but it was probably really only a couple of minutes later when Bunker stopped shooting. And then in the quiet he heard a voice calling out his and Daisy's names.

He dared to raise his head above the grass and saw five uniformed officers fanned out and partially hidden amid the trees. They were coming from the direction of the parking lot.

Martin stood up. Daisy was determined to get to her feet, too, so he helped her up, grimacing at the sight of the arrow still lodged in her arm. "We need a medic," he called out to the police. The officer spoke into a radio collar mic.

Daisy leaned into Martin, resting her head against his chest. He ran his hand over her dark hair, stroking it gently, and then kissed the top of her head.

When he looked up, the cops were continuing their search of the area and a pair of medics headed toward Martin and Daisy.

Thank You, Lord, he prayed silently. Daisy was safe. For now.

At the conclusion of the church service, Martin stole a quick glance at Daisy, seated beside him. Yesterday's attack in Pearce Park had left its mark, literally. Although she'd tried to cover the bruising that had shown up on her face this morning with makeup, he could still see the purplish marks on her forehead and chin.

"Lord, please protect her," he whispered, his voice so quiet that he could barely hear it above the shuffling sounds of congregants standing and the increasing volume of voices as people began to greet and talk to one another.

Daisy glanced at him, offering a beleaguered smile as she reached down to pick up her purse from the floor. When she'd said she wanted to come to church this morning, he hadn't been sure that was a good idea. The men who were after her were ruthless. They could potentially launch a violent attack on her anywhere. Even in a church. Daisy had called the pastor, asking if he wanted her to stay away. He told her she was absolutely welcome, asked her which service she would attend and assured her that they'd be ready for her.

Martin had spotted what appeared to be a plain-clothes cop standing inside the church entrance when he and Daisy had arrived. Another apparent plainclothes cop stood inside the sanctuary. It was sad to know that such a situation was necessary. But the world was a broken, dangerous place. Being a person of faith didn't mean you ignored that truth.

Martin followed Daisy as she exited their row. She stopped at the end of the aisle and let several concerned friends come over and gingerly give her a hug. The arrow that struck her yesterday had lodged in the fleshy part of her arm without causing major blood loss. She'd gotten a few stitches and had a thick wrapping of gauze over the wound.

If things had gone differently yesterday, Martin

could have lost her. While he'd shielded her body with his own as Bunker and Daltrey took shots at them, he'd seen the relief in her eyes when she'd realized Martin was there. He'd heard the raw emotion in her voice, felt the sense of connection between them, and the power of that had been unsettling. It had felt as though the situation had forced them to shove aside every layer of emotional defense they had put in place and made them feel what lay beneath.

Last night Martin hadn't gotten much sleep for a whole host of reasons. He'd worried about Daisy's physical safety and her emotional health. He'd worried about Daltrey and Bunker still running loose in Jameson. The cops hadn't found them and no one knew where the hit men were right now. He'd worried about the chase for the fugitives going on for so long that everyone eventually stopped being as cautious and alert as they needed to be.

He'd also worried that the carefully constructed line he'd drawn between himself and Daisy was getting dangerously blurred.

He would *always* protect her from physical danger. *Always* come running the minute she called. Over the years he'd found it pretty much impossible to set limits on what he'd do for her. But he would not let her fall in love with him. He would not let her think that because of all they were going through together right now, that somehow meant they had a future together.

They didn't.

Martin could hunt down people who were trying to evade justice. He could fight and shoot if he had to. Track an animal or a human being in the wilderness. He was on call as a volunteer helping with high-angle rescue in the event that anyone got injured in the mountains.

But he couldn't have the kind of relationship with Daisy that he knew she wanted. He had too much emotional baggage thanks to his parents. And too many vacant places in his heart and mind where the keys to how to love someone and weather all the ups and downs and still keep things going without bitterly disappointing the other person should be.

If he really loved Daisy, he'd stop allowing himself to savor the feeling of growing closeness between them. He'd do it before he unintentionally hurt her by saying or doing or being the wrong thing for her.

He forced his thoughts away from Daisy and focused them on the fundamentals of their current case instead.

Despite being hit by Martin's bullet, Bunker hadn't left enough of a blood trail for law enforcement to track him. So the injury was likely not life-threatening.

The sheriff's department had gotten a K-9 out there that led them to a forest service access road. There were fresh tire tracks on the dirt and signs that someone had been car camping there. So Daltrey and Bunker were probably hiding out in the park—for the last night, perhaps longer—and maybe this morning one or both of them came into the campground area. For clean water from the tap, maybe. And while they were there they must have seen Daisy and Martin. Perhaps someone in the camp had been an accomplice or had somehow alerted them.

There was no way to be certain. The only thing they knew for a fact right now was that Bunker had altered his appearance. So Daltrey had probably altered his appearance, too.

Daisy finally had talked to everyone who'd come to greet her and she started toward the church foyer with Martin right behind her. They'd come to this service, the earlier of two morning ones, thinking there would be fewer people and Daisy's appearance would draw less attention. Martin could only imagine what it would have been like if they'd shown up for the more popular later-morning service. Daisy not only had a regular presence at church, but she'd helped several of the congregants, using her bounty hunting skills to locate missing people with memory problems as well as a few angry kids who'd run away from home.

"Thank you," Daisy said to the man standing guard inside the foyer as she walked past. The man smiled in response. Martin likewise expressed his gratitude.

The foyer was mostly empty by now and Martin spotted Sheriff Russell just as she called out to Daisy. The sheriff, wearing a lavender dress and heels, stood near a uniformed deputy. A sheriff's department patrol car was visible through the foyer's front windows.

The edgy sense of worry and anxiety that had simmered in the forefront of Martin's mind ever since he'd gotten the original call that Daisy was in trouble flared up. Why were the cops here?

"How are you doing?" The sheriff reached out to take Daisy's hand, her demeanor managing to convey sensitive concern and stony law enforcement officer determination at the same time.

"Is everything all right?" Martin asked, a tense knot already forming in the middle of his gut.

The sheriff nodded. "I'm here for the next service. Unless I get called away." She glanced at the wide expanse of glass at the front of the lobby, and then looked toward the open door of a classroom. "Do you have a minute?" she asked Daisy.

"Of course."

They all moved away from the windows, where Daisy would have been an easy target for anyone driving by, and into the small room.

"I thought you might want a quick update," the sheriff said.

"You've got a lead on Daltrey and Bunker?" Daisy asked.

The hint of eager hopefulness in Daisy's voice nearly broke Martin's heart. Of all the people in the world, why did caring, kindhearted Daisy Lopez have to go through this torment? He shook his head slightly at the pointlessness of the question. How many times had he asked why something terrible had happened to a good person? Many times, often in churches, like this one, during prayer. And during funerals.

Martin could do his best to live a good life. He could pray. He could lean into his faith. But the outcomes were not in Martin's hands. It was simply not his place to understand all and figure everything out. And so often, like now, that reality was very hard to accept.

"No new leads." The sheriff shook her head. "Not yet, I should say. Because we *are* going to find some. We won't quit until we do. And I wanted to tell you about that. We're still following all the details we can on Tony Valens, even though he is deceased, trying to get a handle on where he's been, maybe get some video of him with someone here in town, and we're closely studying any scrap of information that might show us how he became connected with Daltrey and Bunker."

"Do you have any information yet on what kind of vehicle the fugitives are driving?" Daisy asked.

"Unfortunately, no. As of this morning, we didn't have anything new on our stolen vehicle hot sheet. It's possible they grabbed a vehicle sitting in some place where no one would notice it missing for a while. Or they may have bought something from a seller who didn't realize the buyers were fugitives from the law."

"Any chance you've gotten helpful information about their mob buddies from the feds?" Martin asked.

"They have an informant in the Miami mob and they did confirm what Mrs. Lopez overheard, that Daltrey and Bunker have fallen into disfavor with their organized crime bosses and the pressure is on for them to *clean up their mess* before they leave town." She glanced meaningfully at Daisy.

Martin sighed. Instead of things getting better, it seemed like they kept spiraling more and more out of control. At some point, the criminal bosses might decide to send in their own hit team to *clean up the mess*. He glanced at Daisy standing beside him and a chill ran up his spine at the thought of something more happening to her. Even with dedicated law officers from multiple agencies doing their best to help her, how could they possibly capture the thugs and lock them up *and* keep Daisy safe?

"We're still doing our regular beat cop work, as well," the sheriff continued. "The highway patrol is keeping watch on the outskirts of town. Here in Jameson we're in constant contact with car rental companies, motels and security out at the airport. We're staying visible so they know we're after them. Hopefully that will trigger them to panic and make a dumb move. And then we'll have them."

Voices and footsteps in the lobby signaled that people were arriving for the next church service.

"Deputy Flint will see you to your vehicle," the sheriff said, indicating the deputy who'd been quietly standing beside her.

After saying their goodbyes, they walked with the deputy out to Martin's truck and then started the drive back to the bail bonds office. Alvis and Millie usually attended church with Daisy, but they'd decided, for the sake of security, to stay home and go to the evening service instead. Leaving the building empty seemed risky, even with a security system. Daltrey and Bunker were assassins; they knew how to break into buildings, lie in wait, set up ambushes. Actions that once seemed paranoid felt reasonable right now.

"I'm starting to forget what normal life was like," Daisy said as they drove down the road, both of them checking the mirrors at regular intervals to see if they were being followed. "Right now I kind of wish we'd see Daltrey and Bunker tailing us," she added. "Just so we could face them and get this over with." She turned to him. "It's like the feeling in the summer when a thunderstorm is building all day and by afternoon you just want the storm to break and the rain to fall already."

"Yeah, well, I don't really want the hit man thunderstorm to break while we're right here on Edison Avenue in front of Kiki's Knitting Hut," Martin said dryly.

"Name a better place."

"Any place where there aren't any civilians and where we've got the bad guys surrounded by a ring of cops so they can't possibly get away."

"You're right," she said. "That would be better. I'm just getting tired of all of this. And short-tempered."

And in physical pain, Martin thought. She'd been banged up pretty good a couple of times now. "Nobody can blame you for wanting it to be over."

He was taking a circuitous route back to Peak Bail Bonds to make it easier to spot anyone following them, and also because an unpredictable route could foil any attempt at ambushing them on the way back to the office.

"Ah, Fiesta Charlie's," Daisy said as they passed a strip mall with a restaurant. "When we were in high school the onion rings there practically called out to me until I came and got some."

"I remember," Martin said, glancing at the weather-beaten sign showing a taco wearing a top hat, holding a cane and looking like it was dancing. The year he lived in Jameson, it seemed like he and Aaron and Daisy ended up here every Saturday with a crowd of friends. It felt like being surrounded by extended family. And it had given Martin a warm feeling that he had savored after so much time in the chilly atmosphere surrounding his parents at his home in Stone River.

His great-aunt and -uncle who had invited him here for his senior year had done so much more for him than they ever realized. That was ten years ago, and both had since passed away. But they'd left a legacy in his heart. Their faith had shown him a way to live that had helped him survive some dark times.

Daisy and her family had made an impact, too. They were woven into his life and he couldn't imagine carrying on without them.

Seeing Fiesta Charlie's reminded Martin of how hard he'd fallen for Daisy by the end of his senior year. And how that teenage emotion had deepened into more meaningful feelings for her over the years.

But that didn't change the fact that Martin would not be able to make a new, more complicated relationship with Daisy work. It wasn't in him. And if they tried, he knew Daisy would ultimately feel disappointed in him. And the most precious relationship in his life would be gone.

"Now I really want some onion rings," Daisy said. "Quick, pull in before we pass it."

Martin kept going. She was tired and impatient and off her game right now. Daltrey and Bunker had to be at the point where they were willing to do anything to get the situation *cleaned up* and over with. Which meant they could be anywhere. Even behind them in traffic right now, unnoticed. This was not the time to take any chances with Daisy's safety, not even a small one.

"I'll take you home and then I'll come back and get you onion rings," he said.

He would do anything he could to keep Daisy safe. And he would not let this experience ruin his relationship with her. Emotionally, he would cool things down. It was that, or risk losing her forever.

TEN

"This was a good idea," Martin said. "Checking out sporting goods stores might actually get us somewhere."

"Of course it's a good idea," Daisy said, grinning broadly at him when he turned to her. "It's *my* idea." Yesterday's church service had lifted her spirits considerably, leaving her energized and more optimistic than she'd been since the pursuit of Daltrey and Bunker had taken such a personal turn when they'd kidnapped her mother.

Martin rolled his eyes and gave her a begrudging half smile in return. But at least it was something. Last night, and again this morning, when he and Daisy along with Millie and Alvis had been brainstorming ideas on what to do next, Martin had been uncharacteristically quiet. He'd offered ideas related to the fugitives, but other than that he hadn't had much to say.

"Are you mad at me?" she asked as they pulled into the Outdoor Fun parking lot and then sat for a moment as they looked around to make sure the situation was safe before exiting the truck.

"Why would I be mad?" he asked. "What did you do?"

"That's what I'm trying to find out." Walking on eggshells was not Daisy's style. "Have you got a problem with me? Are you sick? Because I'm getting the feeling something is wrong."

He blew out an impatient puff of air. "Yeah. People are trying to *kill* you."

"I know that," she said. "Believe me." She was tempted to point to one of the many injuries on her body. Every time she moved, something hurt. Not cry-out-loud pain. More like an occasional groan. The cut that Tony Valens had made near her collarbone was itching like crazy again. And the amount of makeup she needed to put on her face to hide the bruises made her look like a clown.

So, yeah, she was reminded nearly every waking minute that someone was trying to kill her. But this was Martin, a man who was rarely in a bad mood. And she herself had been pretty frustrated and tired yesterday, so this might be the time for her to cut him a little slack and just drop it.

"I don't see anybody in the parking lot watching us," she said. She grabbed a few of her trusty photo printouts of the two fugitives. The managers at the three other sporting goods stores they'd already visited this morning had promised to post the pictures someplace where shoppers could see them. Hopefully, they would actually do it. Daisy had tweaked Bunker's photo so that it showed him without his mustache and with his hair dyed blond. Daltrey's photo on the other half of the page had a caption saying he'd probably changed his appearance. The pages also contained contact information for Peak Bail Bonds.

Daisy headed straight for the store's front door while

Martin stayed a couple of steps behind her. She could see his reflection in the glass door, his head on a swivel, constantly turning it while scanning their surroundings.

Inside, she walked over to the main counter, introduced herself and Martin as bounty hunters and asked to see the manager. A few minutes later, she was talking to a middle-aged, bearded man in a plaid flannel shirt and khakis. His name was Roger and he followed local news pretty closely, so he was familiar with the hunt for Daltrey and Bunker. And he was more than willing to help in their capture.

"Have you seen the men in here?" Daisy asked. She placed a photo on the counter and Roger picked it up to get a better look. "Hair color and length could be different than what you see in these photos or what has been shown on the news. They also might have added glasses, been speaking with faked accents, things like that to try and throw people off their trail."

Roger slowly shook his head. "I don't remember seeing either of them." He looked up at Daisy. "But we get a lot of customers through here." He gestured toward the cavernous main floor of the store that was filled with everything from tents to baseball bats. "It's possible they've been here. A lot of shoppers come in that I never actually see."

"This one may have bought a hunting-bow setup here," Daisy said, tapping Ivan Bunker's picture.

"Oh, well let's go talk to the lead sales rep in that department."

Roger led the way and introduced Daisy and Martin to Tina, who did indeed remember Ivan Bunker coming into the store. "Yeah, I waited on him. I think it was three or four days ago. Sold him a fiberglass hunting bow, arrows and some gloves. He and his buddy—" she tapped the photo of Daltrey "—bought a couple of sleeping bags, some granola bars and a few other things." She shook her head and looked up at Daisy. "Man, I didn't make the connection between them and the men the cops were looking for. This Daltrey guy has a shaved head, now. Wears dark-rimmed glasses."

"Would you have sales records of the transaction?" she asked, glancing at the store manager. "Something with credit card information."

"They paid in cash," the clerk said. "I was surprised. The total was a little over eight hundred dollars."

"Did either of them flirt or chitchat with you? Tell you where they were going to be camping? What they were going to be doing?" Daisy prodded.

The clerk shook her head. "They didn't have much to say. Just wanted to get their gear and get out of here."

"Okay." Daisy took a breath. "Security video." She glanced around and could see several cameras in the store. "You obviously have security video."

Roger, who'd been waiting nearby all this time, shook his head. "I'm sorry, but we have a strict rule about only releasing store video to law enforcement."

"No problem, I'll let the sheriff know that the fugitives were here." Daisy pulled her phone, which had been found beside Martin's truck near the campground where she must have dropped it, out of her pocket. "Is there any chance you have security cameras in the parking lot?" She hadn't thought to look for any when she and Martin were out there earlier.

Roger nodded. "We do have a couple of cameras out there."

Daisy caught Martin's eye and smiled. A slight smile played across his lips in return. If the outside video had captured Daltrey and Bunker, then they could see what vehicle they'd been driving at the time. Maybe they were still driving the same vehicle now.

Daisy sent a text to the sheriff. Within a couple of minutes, she got a reply telling her that deputies were on the way to the store to talk to the manager.

Daisy thanked the store employees for their help, and then she and Martin left. It would take a while for the sheriff's department to get all the pertinent video, scan it, identify Daltrey and Bunker and make a plan of action based on the information they gleaned. Daisy trusted the sheriff to keep her posted as soon as they learned anything useful. In the meantime, Daisy would go back to chasing down small details, hoping they would eventually lead to a big arrest.

"Where to now?" Martin asked once they were back in his truck.

"Before we go anywhere, don't you want to tell me again what a great idea I had?"

Martin chuckled and shook his head. "No. I do not."

His laugh made Daisy feel better. She tucked her hair behind her ears and rubbed her hands together, energized by the discovery of some fresh new information about the fugitives.

"I've been thinking about Sheriff Russell's comment," Daisy said. "That the combined sheriff and police department task force was still using Tony Valens as a possible starting point to find our fugitives. She's right. Even though he was murdered and can't speak, he might still lead us to useful information if we can figure out where he'd spent most of his time lately and who he spent time with."

"How do you plan to do that?" Martin asked, steering the truck out of the parking lot and onto the road.

"I think it's still a good idea to ask around about him at the university. Justine should be in the office by now. Maybe she can talk to her son again about Valens. Even if Robbie doesn't actually know anything, he might have some guesses as to where we should be looking for people who knew Valens. The fact that he was wearing a university T-shirt when he grabbed me in the alley has me convinced he spent at least some of his time hanging around on the campus."

"Makes sense."

"So, let's go back to the office and then out to the university."

"All right," Martin said. "You're the boss."

"Yes, I am," Daisy said, hoping to get another chuckle out of him. She had her confidence back and it felt good. She hadn't realized how much she'd missed it until now.

Granted, she did feel a shadow of anxiety hovering near the edge of her thoughts. There were a lot of open spaces on the campus. And if someone with bad intent identified her, she could be an easy target to pick off. She took a deep breath and tried to balance the two emotions of optimism and worry. They weren't out of the woods yet. She and Martin needed to be *very* careful. Daltrey and Bunker were still at large. But right now, she felt ready to fight.

* * *

Justine was seated at her desk in the Peak Bail Bonds office when Daisy and Martin arrived back there.

"So, do you think Robbie could get us any information at all about Tony Valens and his connection to the university?" Daisy asked Justine the minute she walked in the door.

Martin was right behind her, pausing to take a look back to see if anyone had followed them to the office or was perhaps driving by slowly out on the street. It was no secret that Daisy worked and lived here, but there was always the possibility that a potential assassin was looking to confirm when she was actually in the building in order to launch an attack.

"I'm asking for Robbie's help again because we just got a good lead on Daltrey and Bunker that we handed over to law enforcement and now I want to keep going and see what else we can dig up," Daisy continued. "I'm pretty certain our fugitives have some kind of network helping them out, one that included Jimmy Nestor and Tony Valens. And Valens was wearing that university T-shirt so I really want to follow that university connection and see where it leads."

Martin felt a smile pass across his lips. Here was the Daisy he so admired, locked on to a target—or in this case two targets—and refusing to let go until they were in custody.

And there, also, was the woman of faith and strength and determination who added such richness and humor and vibrancy to his life. Qualities that he would not risk losing. He held back on his smile, refusing to share the moment with her as she turned to him, eyes flashing, her whole being appearing energized at finally getting some traction in this hunt.

The *moments* shared between him and Daisy needed to happen a little less often. Much as it pained him, he would create some distance between them. Get their relationship back to a *just friends and coworkers* vibe. For the sake of keeping what they had, for the sake of not letting their relationship get overheated and then fall apart when things went back to normal.

Because *normal* for him meant not letting things get too serious. Because as a potential lifelong partner, as a *husband*, he would not have anything worthwhile to offer her.

Justine ran her hand through her red hair. "My son doesn't know who Tony Valens was or where he liked to hang out because Robbie's busy going to class, studying and working at his job at a grocery store. He doesn't have time to socialize or keep track of who's hanging out where." She shook her head. "He'd like to help you but he doesn't know anything."

"Can I talk to him, anyway?" Daisy pulled up a chair and sat close to Justine. "Please."

Martin glanced at Millie, who was sitting at her desk, watching the conversation. Alvis was carrying on his own conversation while pacing in the lobby with his phone to his ear. Steve, who was covering the front counter as usual, appeared to be eavesdropping while tapping away on the laptop in front of him.

"Okay." Justine blew out a breath and some of her defensiveness seemed to vanish. She reached for her personal phone, lying on the desk next to her work phone. "I'll text Robbie. I can't ever remember his schedule and he might be in class right now. I don't know for sure. Do you want me to have him call you?"

"If he could meet me on campus today, whatever time's convenient for him, that would be great," Daisy said. "Maybe he could point me toward an acquaintance who does know something helpful. Tell him if he wants to meet me at the student union building, I'll buy him lunch or an espresso. I'll make it worth his while." Daisy flashed Justine her most winning smile and Martin felt his heart do a small flip.

Justine shook her head and laughed. "Okay, okay. You've sold me on the idea. You can back down now."

"Thanks. I owe you a favor." Daisy sprang up so suddenly that her office chair rolled a couple of feet away and smacked a waste paper basket.

"We've written bonds for a few clients that are college students over the last year or so," Millie said, leaning back in her desk chair and crossing her arms over her chest. "Mostly drug charges or driving under the influence. Maybe we could contact some of them and see what they know, too."

"The more information, the better," Martin said. And the sooner they got this solved, the better. Daisy was feeling a boost in spirits right now, and there was no way he'd begrudge her that. Maybe they finally were closing in on the fugitives. But that meant Daltrey and Bunker would start to feel the heat, and that might make them even more ruthless.

"Tammy Little," Alvis said walking over from the lobby, where he'd finished his phone conversation a couple of minutes ago.

"Good idea," Millie said.

"Tammy's been busted for drug possession on campus a couple of times and we've written bail for her," Daisy explained to Martin. "So far this semester she's stayed out of trouble, but her addiction is real and it's a battle she's still fighting. She comes to church now and then, for services as well as twelve-step meetings. Maybe she'd talk to us, too."

"I've got her contact information in the database," Millie said, tapping on her keyboard. "Let me see if I can get a hold of her."

Daisy turned to Martin. "Meanwhile, let's you and I try to change up our appearance a bit." She glanced down toward her khakis and utility belt, and then back up at him. "Maybe we can find something that makes us look more like college students so people feel more relaxed talking to us."

"Anything that would make you look different than you normally do would make me happy," Martin said.

Daisy raised her eyebrows. "Thanks a lot."

"You know what I mean. You're a target. Let's not make it too easy for anyone to pick you out in a crowd."

"Right." She smiled at him. "I'll do what I can."

And yeah, Martin was willing to change things up so he looked more relaxed. But he wasn't going to *be* relaxed. He was going to be armed and ready. Because an attack could come at any time from any direction.

Dawson University was situated at the southwest edge of Jameson and consisted of several widely spaced buildings set among the low rolling hills. While Martin could easily acknowledge that the layout made for a beautiful campus, it was also true that the sparse scattering of trees made for wide-open spaces where a skilled gunman could target Daisy from a far enough distance that he may not be seen until it was too late.

"Quit turning your head so much," Daisy said from beside him. "I know we need to remain alert, but right now you look like a soldier on patrol in hostile territory and that's not the vibe we're going for."

Martin glanced over and saw the smile on her face. She was teasing him while making her point. She was also professional enough to make certain that anyone watching them, nearby or through a scope from some distance away, would peg them as nothing more than easygoing college students enjoying a fall day made slightly warmer than usual by the bright sunlight in the cloudless blue Montana sky overhead.

Martin wore a dark green hoodie instead of his normal jean jacket, and sneakers instead of boots. Daisy had tucked her long dark hair up into a ball cap and wore her dark gray ballet flats instead of the sturdy lace-up shoes that were good support for chasing down a perp. Neither of them thought they were masking their identity from anyone who knew them. The goal was simply not to stand out starkly among the other students.

Martin had parked his truck as close to the student union as possible, and now they were walking along one of the many concrete paths that crisscrossed the campus. This one led to the three-story student union building with its student government offices, counseling center, student resource office and main dining facility.

"We're right on time," Daisy said after a quick glance at her phone as they approached the building. "Robbie should be getting out of class and stopping by to meet us here on his way to work any minute now." Tammy would be stopping by to meet them, as well, at roughly the same time or perhaps a few minutes later. It depended on when she finished her shift working in the laundry department of student housing.

The main lounge inside the student union was filled with sofas, tables with chairs, and television screens. Martin breathed in the scents of coffee from the nearby coffee bar and food from the dining hall at the other end of the building.

"Let's sit here," Daisy said, moving toward a grouping of padded chairs with a table located by a wall that still afforded a reasonable view of the campus outside through a window opposite them.

She sat down and Martin sat beside her, keeping his gaze moving as he tried to get a look at everyone in the building, checking for anything that might indicate threatening behavior. Like someone staring too long in their direction. Or a person reaching into their pocket to potentially grab a gun.

Daisy was looking around, too, and after a minute or so she lifted her hand to get someone's attention while saying to Martin, "Oh, good. There he is."

A short kid who looked to be in his early twenties with reddish hair like Justine's acknowledged Daisy's wave and walked up to them.

"It's great to see you again," Daisy said to Robbie after introducing him to Martin. "I told your mom I'd buy you a coffee or lunch in return for your help."

Robbie sank down into a chair and dropped his daypack on the ground beside him.

"It's a little late for lunch," Daisy said. "So why don't

you just get whatever you want whenever you want it." She reached into her pocket, pulled out some folded bills and set them on the table in front of him.

"You don't have to do that," Robbie said.

"I want to."

"But I can't help you." Robbie looked intently at Daisy and then at Martin. "I'm sure my mom already told you that."

Daisy cocked her head and flashed him one of her winning smiles. "Robbie." She dropped her chin and leaned closer toward him. "I know you aren't a kid anymore and that you probably don't tell your mom *everything*. You don't want to worry her. I understand that. And that's why I figured I'd come here and talk to you myself."

Martin felt a ripple of appreciation for the way she was setting up the conversation to get him to open up to her. She really was good.

She took a photo of Tony Valens out of the daypack she'd brought with her, placed it on the table so it was facing Robbie and slid it toward him. "Have you ever seen this guy?"

Robbie glanced at the picture and then at Daisy. "No. I've never seen him."

"Are you sure? Take another look. Maybe you've seen him around friends that I'm *not* going to ask you to name. Or maybe you've seen him hanging around campus. See, he's a drug dealer, Robbie. And a kidnapper. He cut me with a knife. Locked me up in a storage closet. And now he's dead." Her tone got sharper with every word, and Martin could see the effect on Robbie as the young man appeared to look at the bruises on Daisy's face.

She took out pictures of Daltrey and Bunker and put them on the table.

"Valens was connected to these people. People who are trying to *kill* me. That's why I want information about him. I'm not looking to bust your friends. Or you. That's not my job. So if you don't know anything, but you have a connection to someone who might be able to give me some information, that would be very helpful."

Martin had been continually shifting his gaze between Robbie and the other people who were sitting and walking in the building. He looked away, and when his gaze settled on Robbie's face again, the young man's eyes were wide and his face was pale. "I don't know anything," he said in a voice stilted with fear. "I don't know what you think or why you think it, but I go to class, I work and I study. That's all. Really."

"Okay," Daisy said, nodding and leaning back in her chair.

Martin could practically feel the disappointment rolling off her.

She sighed heavily. "If you don't know anything, you don't know anything." She picked up the photos and tucked them back into her pack. "Thanks for your time. And if you think of anything, please let me know." She pushed the money she'd offered, which was still on the table, all the way over to him.

He hesitated, then picked it up and put it in his pocket. "Thank you." He stood and Martin watched him walk across the lounge toward a set of double glass doors. He pushed one open and stepped outside.

"Here comes Tammy," Daisy said, sounding a little deflated after her dead-end conversation with Robbie.

"Maybe she can be more helpful." Both she and Martin got to their feet.

A young woman with short dark blond hair and a nose ring walked to their table with a smile on her face until she got closer. Then the smile faded as her gaze lingered on Daisy's face. "I've heard about what happened to you," she said slowly, "but I guess I didn't really realize how bad it was. Those are some serious bruises."

"Don't worry, I'm a quick healer." Daisy made the introductions between Tammy and Martin and then they all sat down.

"To start with, Millie told me you wanted to talk about someone named Tony Valens," Tammy said. "That's not a name I'm familiar with so I don't think I can help you." She looked at Daisy. "And honestly, I'm working hard to stay out of trouble. So I'm careful about who I spend time with these days."

"I believe you." Daisy pulled out the picture of Tony Valens again and put it on the table so Tammy could see it. "This is the man we're asking about."

"Oh, *him*," Tammy said slowly, peering closely at the picture. "He sells drugs on campus." She looked up. "Or he did, anyway. But that's all I know."

"We're interested in absolutely any information that we can get about him," Daisy said. "We'd especially like to know where he used to hang out and who his friends were."

"Can't help you. Sorry." Tammy shook her head. "But you must have gotten some helpful information out of that guy you were just talking to. I saw him leaving as I was walking over to your table."

"Robbie?" Daisy said. "Why would you think Robbie would know anything?"

"Yeah, I guess Robbie. The red-haired dude." She tapped the photo. "I've seen him right here in the student union sitting and talking with this Tony Valens guy lots of times."

ELEVEN

Robbie was long gone when Tammy dropped her bombshell information about his connection to kidnapper and drug dealer Tony Valens. Daisy had left Tammy sitting with Martin as she'd hurried over to the glass door Justine's son had exited through, but he was nowhere in sight. Racing around campus—or to the grocery store where he allegedly worked—felt too much like Daisy could be walking into some kind of setup. Maybe Robbie had given away Daisy's current location to someone who wanted her dead.

Her mind reeled as she tried to take in all of this new information. Resisting the temptation to chase after Robbie that still nudged at her, she walked back across the student union to where Tammy and Martin were still seated. Maybe Tammy was part of some planned attack against Daisy. Maybe she was working with Robbie. Maybe she was lying and Robbie was innocent.

In an instant Daisy had gone from feeling like she was finally getting a handle on the criminal situation she was investigating to fearing that she didn't have any idea at all of what was really going on. A rising sense of panic filled her, tightening her lungs and making it difficult to take a deep breath. Daisy had to quickly tamp it down. *Lord, You have not given me a spirit of fear,* she'd prayed silently. *Please give me Your peace and focus and insight to handle this situation wisely.*

Daisy questioned Tammy further and the young woman seemed to be telling the truth when she described several of the times she'd seen Robbie and Tony here in the student union and also on the outside patio when the weather was good. She explained that she'd originally noticed Valens when she'd seen friends of hers who still used drugs stop and chat with him for a minute. These were friends she cared about but could not currently socialize with for fear of backsliding into addiction. She was certain the *quick chats* were actually drug deals. She'd first seen him when the semester started, around the end of August.

Which was about the time Daltrey and Bunker hit town. After they'd fled Atlanta, but before Peak Bail Bonds had received the request to see if they were hiding near the Idaho-Montana border.

The two hit men weren't known for dealing drugs; their mob connections back in Miami ran an extensive drug supply network. So that might indicate that the hit men were directed by their bosses to come here and start an illicit drug business. That would explain why the pressure would be on them to stay in town and sow an atmosphere of fear and violence rather than simply attempt to vanish like most bail jumpers. And that could also be the impetus behind the order to kill Daisy.

Or, perhaps Daltrey and Bunker decided to branch out on their own with their drug business. Maybe their bosses back east got wind of it and they were unhappy with their murderous employees.

Trying to think of possible motivations and scenarios was something Daisy typically did to help her decide where to search next for the fugitives she was chasing. But at the moment it was only making her anxious again. That anxiety was made worse by her realization that she'd completely misread Justine's son when she'd interviewed him. That kind of mistake could be lethal.

Daisy and Martin thanked Tammy for her help and left the student union, heading for the parking lot.

"I believed Robbie." Daisy shook her head. She knew her admission to Martin wasn't news to him. She just couldn't stop mentally kicking herself a few times. How could she not have seen it? She made her living reading people.

"Yeah, I bought his story, too." Martin fired up the engine in his truck and started making the turns to get them back into town. "But we can't get hung up on that," he added a few moments later. "We've made mistakes and we're going to make more. It would be more helpful to focus on going forward. Do you think his mom knows about his connection with Tony Valens?"

Daisy shook her head. "I don't know. Maybe she's been covering for him, or maybe she has no clue what he's involved in. And if he was hanging around with Tony, he has to be involved in something illicit. I don't for a minute believe that an established drug dealer with a criminal history and a college student are hanging around together on campus because they have similar interests and they like talking about their favorite online game or something."

"I'll bet Robbie is calling or texting his mom about what happened right now to let her know how it went," Martin said. "Even if he has no idea about our conversation with Tammy and that she gave us the connection between him and Tony. Our talk with Robbie had to have made him nervous. And if Tammy noticed him when she walked in, it's possible he noticed her, too.

"Maybe Robbie is connected to those old friends Tammy stays away from now," Martin continued. "If his mom knows what he's mixed up in or if she herself is involved in any way, she might try to get out of the office as soon as she can. Find out exactly what Robbie told you so they can compare notes. And if she's connected to anything illegal she might try to flee town. Or at the least, she won't ever come back into the bail bonds office again. And you'll lose your chance at getting information."

"You're right." Daisy placed a quick call to Millie, made sure she didn't have her phone on speaker and then gave her a brief recap of what had happened.

"Justine has gotten several texts over the last few minutes," Millie said quietly into her phone. Daisy imagined Millie walking away to the other side of the office so she wouldn't be overheard.

"I need to talk to her and I need to talk to Robbie again." This time Daisy wouldn't be so gullible.

"Justine's putting on her sweater," Millie said softly. "I think she's getting ready to go."

"Hurry up!" Daisy snapped at Martin. And then to Millie she said, "Don't let her leave."

Martin pressed harder on the accelerator and began changing lanes to get around slower-moving traffic.

"I can't stop Justine from leaving if she wants to," Millie said into her phone. "We haven't written a bond on her. She's not a bail jumper and we're not the police."

Martin made a sharp turn and Daisy jostled against the passenger door. She bit back a small yelp of pain. The shoulder part of the seat belt had tugged on her body in just the right spot to make her wound from getting shot by the arrow hurt, but she didn't acknowledge that because she didn't want Martin to slow down.

"I know you can't detain Justine against her will," Daisy said into her phone. "Just *please* do something to keep her there a few more minutes. We're almost there."

"Of course," Millie said evenly. "And you try to take a breath and calm down before you get here. You're a bounty hunter and a good one. Use your skills and figure out how you're going to get her to *want* to talk to you."

Millie disconnected. Daisy took in a deep breath and blew it out. Her boss was right. Daisy needed to make sure she handled the situation carefully every step of the way while she hunted for Daltrey and Bunker. No matter how close she got to finding them, if she made a misstep she risked losing everything. Including her life.

"How'd your meeting with Robbie go?" Justine asked Daisy as she walked into the office with Martin closely behind her. Peak Bail Bonds's skip tracer wore a bland smile on her lips. The expression in her blue eyes was flat and guarded.

Fine, Daisy thought, certain that Justine had received some kind of communication about her conversation with Robbie by now. *We can dance around the real topic at hand for a while if you want to.* Daisy would do whatever it took to keep Justine in the office and talking until she finally gave up some information. Her sly behavior already telegraphed that she knew something.

"Robbie didn't really have anything useful to tell me," Daisy said.

Justine's shoulders visibly relaxed, but her bland smile sharpened. "I told you he didn't know anything." She fastened a couple of buttons on her sweater, then opened a desk drawer and pulled out her purse.

"You going somewhere?" Daisy asked casually.

Justine nodded and threw a glance toward Millie. "I was just saying before you got here that I wasn't feeling well. Now that you're back, I think I'll go. Alvis and Steve are out delivering Sammie Carlisle to county lockup. She decided to skip her appointment in court this morning and hang out at her boyfriend's house instead. I stayed here because I didn't want to leave Millie alone. Not with everything that's been going on lately."

She'd probably *really* stayed because she wanted to get a handle on how much Daisy had figured out after meeting with Robbie.

Daisy sat on the edge of the desk across from Justine. From the corner of her eye, she saw Martin walk around behind her and then heard him drop into an office chair, making the springs creak. He was probably pulling his pistol from his holster, keeping his moves subtle and getting ready for anything. Before they'd walked through the office door, he and Daisy had discussed the possibility that Justine had somehow been compromised and now worked for Daltrey and Bunker or the Miami mob.

"That's sad news about Sammie," Daisy said, still maintaining an easygoing, conversational tone. "Behavior like that always makes me wonder what people are thinking. It makes me wonder why people choose to let things spiral out of control like that. Sammie could have gone to court, faced up to whatever she needed to and had a lot less trouble."

"Yeah, well, some people make stupid decisions," Justine said, getting to her feet.

"Are you one of those people who makes stupid decisions?" Daisy asked, deciding the time had come to ramp up the conversation. She'd found a lead on people trying to *kill* her and it had led back to her own office. Keeping her frustration under control was difficult, but she knew she had to do it. She crossed her arms over her chest. "Has Robbie been making stupid decisions?"

"Who are you to talk to me like that?" Justine's eyes narrowed as she ground out the words. "I've worked here for nearly a year." She glanced toward Millie, and then back at Daisy. "You know what kind of person I am. And you know Robbie is a good kid." She shoved her chair against her desk. "I don't know why you suddenly have suspicions about us, but I do know I don't have to listen to this."

"You can talk to us, or you can talk to Sheriff Russell," Daisy said calmly. "Actually, I'm sure you and Robbie are going to be talking to the sheriff, either way. The student union building at the university has security cameras inside and out. Now that the sheriff will know to ask for that security footage—because I intend to tell her everything I know—she'll see Tony Valens with Robbie on numerous occasions, and I have a feeling that's going to open a whole big can of worms. If you talk to us first, show that you're trying to be helpful, that might help you in the long run."

Daisy wasn't certain she wanted to help Justine or Robbie *at all*. But if that was what it took to wrap up this case and get a couple of professional hit men off the streets—and mountain paths—of Jameson, she'd do it.

Justine wordlessly stared at her, her expression angry and defiant, her face turning red. And then, finally, she pulled her chair back out and sat down. "They threatened to kill Robbie if he didn't help them," she said.

"Daltrey and Bunker?" Daisy asked, wondering how in the world Robbie could have ever crossed paths with the Miami mob assassins.

Justine sighed heavily. "Robbie was working hard to get through school." She glanced at Daisy. "He was getting some financial assistance money for tuition, but he needed to keep up his grades to continue receiving it. He needed to work at the grocery store to cover living expenses. He was getting so tired. He needed a boost." Justine looked down at her feet. "So he started taking pills."

Daisy waited to hear the rest. Although it wasn't exactly the same as Tammy's story of developing an addiction, it was similar. A story of somebody trying to find a way to function in a world that felt overwhelming. Thinking they could try *a little something* to take the edge off their anxiety or exhaustion. Believing, at least at the beginning, that they would be able to keep it under control.

Daisy felt sympathy. But at the moment, when she felt pain somewhere in her body every time she moved because people had tried to kill her, multiple times, and were still trying to kill her, the sympathetic feeling wasn't exactly overwhelming.

"So Robbie became addicted to whatever he was taking and then he began assisting Tony Valens with the sales and distribution to help pay for his own habit," Daisy said. The career criminals tended to avoid taking the drugs they sold. The small fries, like Robbie, were easy to control once they were addicted.

"At some point Robbie mentioned to Tony that I worked for a bail bond company," Justine said. "Later, Tony asked Robbie for information on you to help his so-called friends."

"The friends being Daltrey and Bunker," Martin said from his seat at the desk behind Daisy.

"Yeah," Justine said. "And Tony told Robbie that if he didn't get me to help them, they would kill Robbie."

"And it didn't occur to you to tell the cops about this?" Millie said sharply. "Or to tell us?"

"I had no idea that Robbie was mixed up with selling drugs until he told me about the threat and pleaded with me to help him." Justine shook her head. "If I told anyone about this and law enforcement got involved, I knew Robbie could end up facing drug charges. And that having a criminal record could ruin his life forever." She sighed deeply. "I couldn't let that happen. He's practically still a kid."

"But you could help someone try to kill me," Daisy said flatly.

"No," Justine protested, holding up her hands. "*No.* I told Robbie to let them know I could get a list of your confidential informants and that might be of some help.

But that other than that, there wasn't anything I could do. Robbie convinced them that I didn't know your daily schedule and couldn't help them anticipate where you'd be at any specific time. I didn't want you to get hurt. I just wanted to keep my son from getting murdered or going to prison."

So that explained the whole issue of Daisy's informants refusing to help her. And it explained how the bad guys knew who her informants were.

"You sat right here and watched as we tried to figure out how to get leads on finding Daltrey and Bunker. You saw me leave here, knowing people were trying to kill me, and you didn't offer up the information you had." Betrayal and anger churned in her stomach, nearly making Daisy physically sick. "When I came back into the office after my mother had been kidnapped, after I'd been shot at and kidnapped, myself, and after I'd been shot with an *arrow*, you looked me in the eyes and pretended that you didn't know a thing. How could you do that?"

Justine set her jaw. And then said, "I did it to protect my son."

Justine's phone chimed. She lifted it up to glance at the screen and Daisy snatched it out of her hand. "It's Robbie," Daisy said after reading the text. "He wonders why you haven't met up with him yet. He's outside and he sees that your car is still here."

Come into the office, Daisy typed into the phone, and then she hit Send.

"Give me my phone back," Justine snapped.

Daisy held on to the phone. "I will eventually."

Robbie showed up at the front door, which was still

being kept locked for security's sake, a couple of minutes later. Martin got up to let him in and followed him closely as he walked into the office toward Daisy and Justine.

"Hey, Mom," Robbie greeted Justine uncertainly. "What's going on?"

Justine explained to him that Daisy knew everything.

"None of this is my mom's fault," Robbie blurted out when she was finished talking. He turned to Daisy, tears in his eyes. "This is all on me."

"It's all on both of you," Millie said, having stood up and walked a little closer.

Millie was probably concerned that Robbie was armed. Or that he might now act out violently. Daisy's boss was a good-hearted woman of advanced years, but she could still break out some pretty good moves if people who were upset decided to get physical. The emotion in the room was high, and both Justine and Robbie were looking anxious and unstable. Experience had taught Daisy that people were capable of anything if they thought they were about to be arrested.

"What if I give you some information that might help you out?" Robbie asked, nervously licking his lips. "Would you let my mom go? Let her stay out of this?"

"What kind of information?" Justine asked, eyebrows raised.

"First, before I say anything, I want to make a deal. You don't let my mom get charged with anything."

"I can't make any kind of deal," Daisy said. "That's up to cops and prosecutors. But I can tell them that you helped us. If, in fact, you do help us."

"I overhead some stuff I wasn't supposed to," Robbie

finally blurted out after nearly a minute of silence. "I was at Tony's apartment. It was at night on the day that he saw you and grabbed you in the old part of town in the alley. Daltrey and Bunker came by the apartment to talk to him about what had happened and what they wanted to do with you. They weren't there for long. I think they were just looking for a safe place to mentally regroup before deciding their next move.

"Beau Daltrey was really upset. He was on his phone yelling at someone, demanding they help him. He had the volume turned up loud enough that I could hear the other side of the conversation. It sounded like his mob friends were sending a couple of their guys to Jameson by plane. Guys who are known by the FBI. Not wanted criminals, but men who are known to be mob thugs. The idea is that once they arrive at the airport in Jameson, the cops will latch onto them and tail them, hoping to find Daltrey and Bunker. And the thugs will lead them on a wild-goose chase.

"In reality, those thugs are decoys. The same flight will have a man and woman on it who are not known criminals. But they are connected to the mob. They'll be dressed in flannels and jeans so they'll blend in with a lot of other people on the flight. *Those* two are the people who will actually meet up with Daltrey and Bunker and help them escape town without leaving a trail behind them."

Daisy turned to Martin, hoping to see whether or not he believed Robbie's story. Because she'd believed Robbie earlier today when he was lying to her. Maybe he was lying to her now. Normally, she trusted her gut. But right now she didn't. What if all of this was just another, more elaborate lie? What if she acted on it and it led to an ambush?

Martin met Daisy's gaze and raised his eyebrows slightly. She knew Martin well enough to read the expression. He questioned what Robbie said, but hadn't completely decided that he disbelieved him, either.

"Why go through this elaborate process to get them out of town?" Millie asked Robbie. "Why didn't Daltrey and Bunker just hire Tony Valens to drive them out of town? Or hire you to drive, for that matter?"

Robbie shrugged.

"Maybe they don't trust anyone other than their mob friends," Daisy said. "Daltrey and Bunker were found when they were hiding near Atlanta. Maybe they were afraid to leave a trail and get found again." She turned to Robbie. "When was all of this supposed to happen?"

"They mentioned Tuesday," Robbie said. "Maybe they meant tomorrow Tuesday, but I don't know for certain."

"We're going to need to tell the sheriff about this so she can set up countermeasures," Daisy said to Millie.

"If you're going to tell the cops so they can sweep in and bust everybody, you might as well paint a target on my back," Robbie said. "If Beau Daltrey and Ivan Bunker get captured by the police after their organized buddies fly into town, one or both of them will eventually remember seeing me in Tony's apartment. They'll put everything together and figure out I was the one who ultimately got the information to the police. Even if they're locked up, they'll get the information to their bosses and then the mob will come after me for revenge."

Justine burst into tears and stood up to wrap her arms around her son.

Martin moved to Daisy. "Maybe we can figure something out. Find a way to capture Daltrey and Bunker without there being dozens of law enforcement officers in place after their criminal friends arrive at the airport so it isn't so obvious that Robbie informed on them. He and his mom will still have to ultimately face up to what they've done, but that way they won't be targeted by the mob and they won't have to pay for their bad decisions with their lives."

Daisy nodded. She was still angry, but she knew that eventually, with prayer, she would get her emotions sorted out. She could do her job and still show mercy. Because mercy had been shown to her so many times in her life. Granted, her mistakes hadn't been as extreme as what Robbie and Justine had done. But she was still imperfect, like anyone else.

"I think it's time for you to call in your reinforcements at Rock Solid Bail Bonds," she said quietly to Martin. "We're going to need more bounty hunters."

"I'll call Harry and Leon tonight."

Daisy took in a deep breath and blew it out. The time to get this case wrapped up might finally be at hand. She just hoped that everyone working the case would live through it.

TWELVE

"The plane has been parked at the gate for fifteen minutes," Martin said, with a glance at Daisy sitting beside him in his truck. "Passengers should be getting off and walking through the terminal doors any minute now. If our targets aren't on this flight, then we know that Robbie's tip didn't pay off."

Jameson's small regional airport had only two scheduled inbound flights per day, both of them small commuter planes arriving from Seattle or Portland. The morning flight had been nearly empty, and no one who deplaned had fit the profile the bounty hunters were looking for. So now, twelve hours later at seven in the evening, they were back watching the arriving passengers again. They were also watching the parking lot for Daltrey and Bunker, just in case they'd decided to show up at the airport even though, according to Robbie's story, that wasn't part of the plan. The two bail-jumping hit men had been unpredictable from the beginning. There was no reason to assume that would stop now.

"Get ready," Martin said into his phone.

"I was born ready," the deep voice of Leon Bragg

came back through the speaker. "I'm ready while you're still sleeping."

Daisy turned toward Martin, rolled her eyes and laughed.

Leon Bragg and Harry Orlansky, Martin's fellow bounty hunters from Stone River, had arrived at the Peak Bail Bonds office well before sunup this morning. Right now they sat in a pickup truck parked near the lot's exit, ready to follow the decoy mob men. The feds were already watching flight manifests in an attempt to find the fugitives. Since there was currently a regional manhunt underway for two hit men connected to the Miami mob, the bounty hunters assumed that local law enforcement would be alerted by the feds when the decoy mobsters arrived. And that local law enforcement would follow them in hopes of being led to fugitives Daltrey and Bunker. Leon and Harry were going to tail the decoys, as well, just in case that assumption was wrong, or law enforcement ended up needing some extra help.

Since the decoys were intending to attract the attention of the law, they would probably try *not* to blend in with everyone else. They'd probably look like stereotypical mob guys—heavily muscled, stylish clothes, maybe some flashy jewelry. Or something equally obvious. And when the bounty hunters saw them, they'd know to also look for the more understated man-and-woman team who were really there to extract the fugitives. Daisy and Martin would be following that team.

People began to exit through the terminal doors. Two men walked out who fit the profile of the obvious mob decoys, right down to the leather jackets and gold chains.

"Think they're overdoing it a bit?" Martin asked.

"Big-city people assume small-town folks are dumb." Daisy shook her head. "This will just make it that much sweeter when we take them all down."

"I'm convinced these are our guys," Harry Orlansky said over the phone line they'd kept open.

"I can't help thinking that if we put a leather jacket on you and some gold jewelry, you'd look like a mobster, too," Martin responded.

On the other end, in the background, he could hear the deep sound of Leon chuckling.

"Me?" Harry said. "What about Leon? He looks more like a thug than I do."

"Okay, I think these two are the actual extraction team here to get our fugitives out of town," Daisy said to Martin.

A man and woman walked out of the terminal and, like the mobster decoys who were not far away from them, they stood on the sidewalk looking around like they were trying to get their bearings. Each of them toted just one small piece of carry-on luggage.

There was a rental car counter in the terminal that stayed open for a couple of hours around the time that flights arrived or departed. The vehicles they rented out were parked in ten marked stalls on the north end of the airport parking lot. The mob guys walked in that direction and the couple headed that way, as well.

As they got into respective rental cars, the woman and one of the decoy mobsters glanced over at one another. In Martin's opinion, they held the glance a little longer than anyone would who was simply looking around. Bounty hunting was all about judgment and making calls when you didn't have much in the way of irrefutable facts.

The decoys backed their car out first and made the turns that would lead to the service road and ultimately to the highway.

"We're ready to roll," Harry said over the phone. He and Leon stayed in place as the mobster car drove by. They waited a few minutes before pulling out into the traffic that was exiting the airport and beginning to follow them.

"Keep an eye out for the unmarked cop cars that should be tailing them," Daisy said into the phone. "And maintain your distance. You don't want to get in their way."

"Copy that," Harry replied. "We'll maintain a low profile."

"And we will do the same," Martin replied as the mob couple backed their car out of the parking spot and headed toward the service road. He waited a couple of minutes before starting to follow them. "Pay close attention to what I do. You might learn something," he said to Daisy. They picked up speed as the mob couple got onto the highway headed toward town and started accelerating.

Daisy made a loud scoffing sound. And while Martin couldn't see her rolling her eyes, he knew she was doing it. "That'll be the day," she said, barely keeping the laughter out of her voice. "But we do make a good team," she added a minute later.

Yeah, Martin thought. *We really do*.

"Our mob guys are turning off the highway at the edge of town," Harry said over the open phone line. "It looks like at least one unmarked cop car is following them."

"Good," Daisy said. "Meanwhile, our couple is staying in the inside lane, so I guess we're going to pass by the exit you're turning off on and we're going into the center of town."

"Well, it looks like Daltrey and Bunker aren't hiding at Pearce Park anymore," she said to Martin a few minutes later as the mob couple passed the exit leading to the park and kept on going.

"Our mob guys went to the old Safari Motel," Harry said over the phone line they were still keeping open. "They're going straight to a room without stopping by the front office. Looks like they're meeting somebody here."

"What about the vehicle you thought was an undercover cop car?" Martin asked.

"It's here. They're actually in the parking lot. We're across the road."

"Stay back and stay cautious," Martin said. "I hope you aren't being led into a trap."

"I hope we aren't being led into a trap, either," Daisy said as they continued down the highway. They were now passing through the center of town, and the mob couple they were following showed no signs of slowing.

They'd driven a couple of miles with no one talking, and then the muted sound of voices came through the phone they'd been using to stay in touch with Harry and Leon. One of the voices did not sound at all like either of the two bounty hunters. And then the call dropped.

Martin's heart started hammering in his chest. He reached for his phone, but Daisy beat him to it. Since the phone was already on speaker, he could hear as she tried to reconnect the call, but the phone went to Harry's voice mail instead.

"They might not be in trouble," Daisy said calmly. But she kept redialing. She was worried, too.

Martin's thoughts raced as he started to imagine what could be happening. Harry and Leon were more than just fellow bounty hunters to him. They were like family. "They can handle themselves," he said, more to calm himself than to impart information to Daisy. Still, there was a real possibility that they were in trouble. *Serious* trouble.

Daisy kept tapping the screen, trying to reconnect with the bounty hunters. Martin was at the point of telling her to call 9-1-1 when Harry finally answered. "The cops are here," he said.

The relief Martin felt nearly made him slump over the steering wheel.

"The undercover cops spotted us and wanted to know who we were. Told us to turn off the phone." He blew out a breath. "They got a lot of backup and then gained entrance to the motel room with the mob guys. No one else was in the room, just the two men we saw at the airport. Some of the cops are questioning them about their connection to Daltrey and Bunker. The rest are checking all the rooms to see if the fugitives are here somewhere.

"Mostly likely, as you and Daisy suggested, all of this was meant to divert the cops' attention while the mob couple hooks up with the fugitives and they all hightail it out of town."

Raindrops began to fall on the windshield. The weather was already cold. If the temperature dropped much more, the rain would turn to snow. The mob couple exited the highway.

"What's going on with your end of the chase?" Harry asked. "Do you have any information for me to pass on to the cops?"

"Not yet," Martin answered. "We don't know our mob couple's ultimate destination, and if there are suddenly a lot of cop cars in their vicinity, they might get spooked and run. If that happens, we've lost everything."

He glanced at Daisy, who nodded in agreement.

"Why don't you and Leon start heading in our direction," Martin said. He gave them the street they were now on and the direction they were headed. They disconnected the call.

The mob couple suddenly sped up. This stretch of road had some businesses plus the entrance to a small industrial park, so Martin could keep up with them without being too obvious. But just a few miles ahead, town ended and countryside began. If the mob couple went much farther, Martin's truck following them in the dark would be much more noticeable.

They were heading up a hill. Without signaling, the car made a sudden sharp turn onto a side street.

"Do you think they've figured out we're following them?" Daisy asked.

"I don't know." If Martin made the turn directly behind them, he'd show his hand. But if he didn't make the turn, he risked losing them.

"Go straight," Daisy said as she turned in her seat and craned her neck to look back at the car. There was a vacant lot on the corner so she could see them driving for a short distance. "They aren't driving fast now," she said. "If they were worried about being followed, I don't think they're worried now. Turn right on the next street and circle back. There aren't a lot of roads up here. There aren't that many places they could go."

Martin made a right turn. And then another. He was quickly within the general area of where the car should be. But it was nowhere in sight. His heart sank. They could not lose these people. They were part of the Miami mob, an organized crime syndicate looking for revenge. What if they got away, teamed up with Daltrey and Bunker, and the four of them joined forces to kill Daisy?

"Let's drive around and look for them," Daisy said.

The mob couple's car had disappeared down a street in the industrial park. The expansive property was a patchwork of warehouses, vacant lots, manufacturing businesses and storage buildings. Martin drove down a street that turned out to be a dead end. He made a U-turn, quickly backtracked and then turned down another street.

Daisy scanned the cars parked at the curb, in the lots adjacent to the businesses and moving in traffic, desperately trying to find where the couple went. "They could have pulled into a building with a delivery bay and pulled the door closed," she said. "If they did, we'll never find them."

"You think they have a connection with a business out here?" Martin asked.

"I have no idea." Daisy shook her head. "But it's not going to help if we get stuck overthinking things. What do we *know*?"

Martin turned onto another street while Daisy looked around.

"We know they aren't from around here," she said, answering her own question. "Assuming that the couple in the car are who we think they are and we didn't make a colossal mistake."

"Where are you going with that train of thought?" Martin asked.

"If they didn't disappear into one of these buildings, we might still be able to find them. Even with GPS, they could be lost if they aren't from around here. Maybe they're supposed to meet up with Daltrey and Bunker and they don't have a specific address. Maybe they have a general idea of where they're supposed to be but they're confused."

"Okay, well, we've driven down every little road in this industrial park," Martin said. "Now what?"

"Maybe the turn into the industrial park was a mistake. Let's get back onto the main road and follow it until it turns into countryside. Maybe that's where they were headed. It's worth a try."

Martin returned to the main street, following it as the businesses on the side started to thin out until there was only farmland alongside the road and forest on the surrounding jagged hills. Traffic was nearly nonexistent, but there were moving headlights in a field in the distance.

Daisy grabbed the night-vision binoculars Martin kept in the truck and held them up to her eyes to get a better view. "I think it might be the same car the mob couple was driving," she said. "I can't see the license plate to be sure. It looks like they turned off onto some farm access road."

"Daltrey and Bunker have been out of sight for the last three days," Martin said. "They could have found a place to lie low out here in the country. Maybe a farmer rented them a couple of rooms or something."

They reached the farm road and Martin killed the headlights on his truck before making the turn so the bad guys wouldn't see them coming. This wasn't Daisy's first time barreling down a road in the dark in pursuit of fugitives, but the experience was still unnerving. The light rain was still falling and the road was turning boggy. She kept the binoculars to her eyes, but it was hard to see detail with all the jostling.

"Tell me if there's a big rock or pothole or animal I need to see," Martin said. "Or if you see anybody hidden by the road waiting for us."

"Right." That was always a concern when pursuing someone. That they might have lured you into a trap.

They passed through a cluster of trees lining the road. Beyond that point the road curved to the left. There was another cluster of trees up ahead and beside them were a barn and a shelter next to it with a tractor parked underneath. This late in the year harvest was wrapped up and there would be no pressing reason for a farmer to be out here after dark in the rain.

"There they are," Daisy said after they drove a little farther.

Martin tapped the brakes. The mob couple's car was in front of the closed-up barn, engine idling, raindrops visible in the beam from the headlights shining on two men. One of the men carried a duffel bag.

"It's Daltrey and Bunker," Daisy said, able to see them clearly through the binoculars.

They were still a good half mile away. Martin steered his truck across the overturned soil and stopped when they reached another cluster of trees that offered cover.

"I can't wait to bust them," Daisy said, indulging in a wide smile even though the bad guys weren't within reach just yet.

"Let me tell Harry and Leon where we are," Martin said. "As soon as they get here, we can surround these thugs and take them all down. But if our criminals try to drive away before Harry and Leon get here, we've got to call the cops. We can't risk losing them again."

"I agree."

Martin quickly placed the call.

The doors to the idling car opened. The man and woman from the airport got out and walked toward Daltrey and Bunker. It looked like the four of them exchanged a few words. Daisy rolled her window down, but she couldn't make out what they were saying.

Ivan Bunker set the long duffel bag he'd been carrying on the ground, unzipped it and pulled out a pistol and handed it to the woman. Then he reached into the bag again and handed her what looked like an additional box of ammunition. Daisy couldn't see for certain, because the headlights created an excess of light that made the night-vision binoculars less helpful.

"Makes sense the fugitives who were already here would bring guns to the new arrivals," Martin said. "They couldn't bring their pistols on the plane with them. And what's a mobster without a weapon?"

The woman checked her gun. Apparently it was already loaded. She tucked it into her waistband.

Bunker did the same thing again with the man, taking a pistol out of the duffel bag and handing it over. The man likewise popped out the clip, checked it and then popped it back in. Then he tucked the gun into his waistband. Bunker reached into the duffel bag one more time and pulled out a rifle with a scope, followed by a box of ammunition.

"They're arming up pretty heavily for people who flew into town only to drive Daltrey and Bunker out of here," Daisy said. "You think they anticipate a run-in with the cops?"

"Maybe. Or maybe they plan to come after you."

Daisy felt for the gun she'd borrowed from Millie after Ivan Bunker took hers at Pearce Park and made sure it was within reach. Harry and Leon needed to hurry up and get here. She was looking forward to feeling a sense of relief when these dangerous people were finally locked up.

Bunker picked up the duffel bag, turned it over and shook it, as if checking to make certain he hadn't left anything in inside.

Meanwhile the man took the rifle and laid it crosswise on the hood of the car. When he turned back around, Bunker tossed the empty duffel bag on the ground. The woman pulled the pistol from her waist-band, stepped forward and shot Bunker twice in the head at close range. He dropped to the ground. The wounds were obviously fatal.

For the first few seconds after the shots were fired, Daisy felt like her own heart had stopped beating.

Martin was already on his phone, calling 9-1-1 to report the murder.

Daisy's gaze was locked on the thugs in front of her. Daltrey barely batted an eye. Had he known his part-ner was going to be murdered? Or had his life as a pro-fessional hit man made him blasé around death? As a bounty hunter, Daisy had come across some vile and heartless people. She probably shouldn't be shocked by depraved behavior anymore. But she was.

Martin disconnected from his call. "The cops are on their way."

"Let's hold tight until somebody gets here," Daisy said. She nodded toward the direction of the bad guys. "They've got us outnumbered, plus they've got that long rifle. They could aim accurately at us from a distance. That's not good."

"I think they have that rifle because they plan to come after you before they leave town," Martin said. "My guess is that they plan to go from here to Peak Bail Bonds where they intend to find you, shoot you and then leave town. By the time the authorities could identify them as the shooters and distribute photos on-line, they could be long gone."

"Taking Beau Daltrey with them," she said.

"Or not," Martin said grimly. "They could just be keeping him alive until he can help them find you."

That would wrap up the whole problem for the mob. Give them a clean break.

Daltrey pulled open the door and got into the back seat of the mob couple's car. He didn't even have a suitcase with him. The couple got into the car, as well.

"They're leaving," Daisy said, just as the car backed out and swung around, the sweep of its headlights flickering through the trees.

"If they see us, we're in a world of hurt," Martin said, pulling his gun out of his holster.

"Slide down out of sight," Daisy said, likewise gripping her weapon. "If they don't see us in here, they might think someone just left a truck parked near the barn."

Daisy dropped down to the floorboard. Martin lay down across the bench seat.

Through the open window, Daisy could hear the tires rolling over the rocks and mud as they slowly drove by. Her heart hammered rapidly in her chest, and the heel of her hand holding the gun felt sweaty.

She looked up and locked eyes with Martin. There was enough light that she could see his face. And then, because he was Martin, he smiled at her. Even in the midst of fearing for her life, her heart felt like it broke into a million pieces. The intensity of the moment had drawn out some real truth. And the truth was she loved Martin. She had for a long time. She always would. And she would never, ever be able to marry anyone else. She knew that now as well as she knew her own name. She couldn't kid herself anymore.

The car rolled by and Daisy let out a sigh of relief. Either they didn't see Martin's truck, or, as she'd hoped, they'd seen the parked truck and hadn't realized it was there when they drove by the first time. The mobsters might be good at their jobs, but they weren't perfect.

"Where are the cops?" Daisy said as she climbed back up onto the bench seat. "And Harry and Leon, why aren't they here yet?"

"I'm sure they're getting here as fast as they can," Martin said, "but we can't stay and wait for them. We've got to follow the criminals. If they get away they will find you and kill you."

"And if you're right, and they're headed for the Peak Bail Bonds office, Alvis and Millie are in danger."

"I'm afraid so," Martin said.

"All right." Daisy gestured toward the car full of mobsters that was disappearing down the farm road. "Let's go after them."

THIRTEEN

Martin slowly drove forward, following the mobster car as it headed down the farm access road and toward the main road. Daisy looked across the dark fallow field, hoping to see the red and blue flashing lights that would indicate help was here. She didn't see anything. Nor did she hear sirens, even though she still had her window down a little despite the literally freezing temperature. The light rain that was falling earlier was now dropping down as icy flakes.

The mob car reached the intersection with the main, paved road and stopped. Martin also hit the brakes. Daisy held her breath. She waited to see if the car turned right, toward the wilderness and escape into southern Montana and potentially anywhere in the country, or left, and back toward the outskirts of Jameson.

The car turned left, toward town.

"They aren't going to leave until they finish tying up loose ends," Martin said grimly.

Yeah. And that meant killing Daisy and anyone who got in their way while they tried to do it. Like Alvis and Millie. She placed a quick call to Millie, explaining to

her what was happening and warning that she and Alvis
should be ready for anything. Then, after telling her she
had to go, she disconnected.

"I'm going to have to let them get a little ahead of
us," Martin said as the mob car started picking up speed
and ascended the slight hill. "There's traffic on the main
road so I need to use my headlights. I don't want to be
close behind them when I turn them on. They might
notice and realize they've been followed."

"Just stay close enough that I don't lose sight of
them," Daisy said, grabbing hold of the night-vision
binoculars just in case. She would *not* lose these criminals again.

Martin gave it a few seconds, then flicked on his
headlights and turned onto the highway. After driving
in the darkness, it felt like they'd suddenly turned on
a spotlight. Daisy's gut tightened with anxiety. These
mobsters were pros. They had to know how to watch for
tails. It made sense that they hadn't spotted Martin and
Daisy following them from the airport because there'd
been a fair amount traffic around them. But here, now,
with only sparse traffic, the sudden illumination of the
headlights might have shown up in the rearview mirror
and caught the driver's attention.

Daisy prayed that hadn't happened. Because if it had,
the driver would take evasive maneuvers and get away
in the darkness. And Daisy and everyone she cared
about would be in danger.

"They're speeding up," Martin said as the car started
up the hill ahead of them.

"Could be coincidence," Daisy said. "Maybe not.

Maybe they've spotted us. Forget about being subtle. You've got to speed up, too. We can't risk losing them."

They passed by a gas station with a convenience store and a small strip mall. They were out of the countryside and back on the edge of town now. Up ahead, the road was part of the main drag for this section of town with all of its interconnecting side streets where the mobsters could turn multiple times until Martin and Daisy lost track of them.

Martin's phone rang. Caller ID showed that it was his fellow bounty hunter Harry Orlansky. "What?" Martin barked, answering with the truck's hands-free device.

"We're close to your location," Harry answered. "Where exactly are you?"

"Northbound heading into town." Martin gave him the specifics, including a couple of cross streets that they'd soon be approaching. "We're following our two from the airport plus they've picked up Daltrey. Bunker's dead. They shot him."

Daisy heard Harry sigh heavily over the phone. "We'll be ready for them."

"I need to call 9-1-1 and let them know exactly where we are right now," Daisy said to Martin. "They might have already arrived at the barn where you called in Bunker's murder." She reached for her phone without taking her eyes off the car ahead of them. The mobsters' sedan peaked the top of the hill and then dropped out of sight.

Martin hit the gas to catch up with them.

Daisy tapped 9-1-1 on her phone just as Martin's truck crested the hill and she heard a loud popping sound followed by a couple more. Bullets blew three holes through the windshield, one of them blasting all the way through and out the back window, the other two hitting the interior and sending fragments of cloth and plastic flying.

"Get down!" Martin yelled, swerving the truck to the right.

Daisy heard two more bullets *clink* as they hit the body of the truck. She slid down slightly, but not so far that she couldn't see. She grabbed her pistol and hit the button to roll her window down farther. If they were going to force her to respond with lethal force, she'd do it.

"What's going on?" Harry called out through the truck's speaker.

At the same time, Daisy could hear the insistent voice of the 9-1-1 operator on her own phone. She'd dropped it, and right now was not a good time to pick it up. "We're being shot at," she called out, giving the location just before her phone slid to the floor and out of reach.

"I've got to stay on them," Martin said to Daisy. "Capturing them is the only way to keep you safe."

"I know," she snapped, waving at him to speed up. *"Go!"*

The safety glass on the truck's windshield held together despite the holes in it and the road ahead was visible through the spiderweb of cracks.

The mob car was several car lengths ahead of them, moving fast.

They were well into town now, with streetlights making things visible as they sped past stores and businesses. The recklessness of the mobsters had Daisy nervous not just for Martin and herself, but for innocent bystanders, as well.

"We're turning off the highway and headed toward you right now," Harry said over the speaker, startling Daisy, who'd forgotten about the open phone line.

"They'll be coming up on you pretty fast," Martin said. "Do what you can to slow them down until the cops can show up, but be careful. They aren't afraid to shoot."

"Yeah, we heard," Harry said dryly.

Martin gave them a quick description of the vehicle so they'd know exactly what they were looking for.

Brake lights flared ahead of them. The mob car was slowing down and Martin's truck was getting close.

Daisy got a sick feeling in the pit of her stomach as Beau Daltrey leaned his upper body out of the rear passenger window, turned toward them and started firing.

Martin slammed on the brakes as a bullet took out the passenger side mirror, sending fragments of broken mirror flying toward Daisy, slicing the skin on her right cheek.

They were near a grocery store with people in the parking lot who were in danger of being struck by a stray bullet.

"We've got to stop pursuing them," Daisy said, nearly choking on the words as she said them. "An innocent bystander could get hurt."

"I'm sorry," Martin said. "I know it's the right thing to do." He sighed heavily. The call with Harry had dropped and now Martin punched the screen to reconnect to his fellow bounty hunter. "Bad guys are heading straight for you," he said as soon as Harry answered. "We've had to fall back. Too dangerous for civilians."

"We're on it," Harry answered. "I hear sirens. I think the cops are close. With the sudden temperature drop and black ice forming on the road, people are sliding and it's slowing down traffic." That must be why the cops weren't here yet.

As Martin slowed down, the bad guys sped away. But then the driver hit the brakes. He flipped a U-turn and then started to accelerate, crossing over the yellow line in the center of the street so that they were now barreling directly toward Daisy and Martin.

Beau Daltrey leaned out of the back driver's-side window pointing a gun at them. The mob woman leaned out of the front window on the passenger side also pointing a gun at them.

"They want to kill me here and now," Daisy said, her voice shaky with adrenaline and fear.

"That's not going to happen," Martin said. "I've got to lead them away from all these people. These idiots don't care who they hit."

Bullets started flying at them before Martin could turn onto a side street.

Daisy didn't want to add to the danger, but as she saw Daltrey take aim at her, she had no choice. She leaned out the window and returned fire.

Her bullet hit the driver and he slumped over the steering wheel. The woman reached over and grabbed the collar of his shirt, pulling him away from the steering wheel. His weight shifted, and the car sped up and smashed into the truck on Martin's side, glancing off it and then spinning into a car that had pulled over to the curb and was filled with terrified-looking occupants.

The airbags in the truck deployed, stunning Daisy for a moment, but she quickly regained her wits and pushed the now-deflating bag out of the way.

"You okay?" Martin called out as he impatiently tried to move his airbag aside.

"Yes."

Ahead of them, a big green pickup truck slid to a stop on the icy road behind the mobster car. Two big guys got out and approached the car with guns drawn.

"Harry and Leon," Daisy said, relief coloring her voice.

"About time they got here," Martin snapped.

The slushy rain was falling harder now. They'd come to a stop away from a streetlight and it was hard to see much. One of the headlights on Martin's truck was broken. Both headlights were broken on the mob car.

Impatient to get out and make her capture, Daisy unfastened her seat belt and pushed open her door. A sharp pain stabbed at her, and she yelped and froze for a second. The crash didn't seem to have created any new injuries, but it had aggravated all the ones she already had.

"Wait here for the medics to arrive," Martin said, drawing his weapon and kicking his dented door to get it to open. He moved toward the civilian car, calling out to them and asking if anybody was hurt.

Daisy didn't want to wait. She got out of the truck and moved toward the mobster car. The front looked pretty bashed up. Martin's truck had definitely been the more solid vehicle. Harry and Leon were already beside it, guns drawn, with car doors pulled open.

She moved toward the car with her gun drawn, sucking in a shallow breath with each painful movement of her arrow-injured arm. Slush covered the windshield, blocking her view. She was determined to get a look inside. She wanted to see Beau Daltrey up close before the cops arrived and carted him away.

Harry and Leon each gave her a nod of acknowledgment as she approached.

She walked around the open driver's-side door and saw the driver sitting up, slump-shouldered and looking disoriented, hands on the steering wheel. There was a bullet hole in the windshield where the rearview mirror should have been anchored and the mirror was missing. When she'd fired at the car, the bullet must have hit the mirror and the mirror hit the man's head. In the passenger seat, the woman had her hands on the dashboard. Having the perpetrators keep their hands in view was standard procedure.

Daisy then shifted her gaze toward the back seat. It was empty.

No. Beau Daltrey *had* to be back there. Maybe he was lying on the floor. Daisy hurried around to the rear door for a better look.

"Where'd he go?" Daisy asked Leon since he was closest to her.

The bounty hunter shook his head. "No one's left the scene since I got here."

In the front seat, the woman started to laugh. It was a harsh, belittling sound that made Daisy's skin crawl.

"You're marked for assassination," the woman said. "There's not a thing you can do to stop it."

Daisy took a step back and looked around. *Where could he have gone?*

Where would she have gone if she'd wanted to escape in the confused aftermath of the car wreck? She'd have headed toward the darkened side of the street opposite where Martin and a few good Samaritans were helping the civilians in the car that had been struck.

Daisy began to jog in that direction, wincing at the pain. Her injuries hurt, but she wasn't going to let them stop her now. She had her pistol drawn and her senses on high alert, sharpened by the awareness that the man she was now tracking on foot was a professional hit man. He knew how to lure a pursuer into a deadly trap.

A narrow alleyway cut between two buildings. Daisy thought she saw a flicker of movement over there and she headed in that direction, attempting to set a pace between a foolhardy chase and a slow trek that could cause her to lose him.

The alley was dark, but a little bit of illumination from the main street spilled over in this direction, and there were a couple of single bulbs burning by the back exits of businesses. That still left plenty of shadow draped across steps, stoops, belowground entrance wells and garbage cans.

She scanned the area as best she could as she continued moving. The alley wasn't very long. She could see where a street intersected with it a few yards ahead. A couple of cars drove by on that street. If she were a mob assassin determined to avoid arrest, she'd run for that street and steal a car. Maybe shove a gun in the face of a driver and force them to drive away from the hot spot where the cops were now converging. Once safely away from capture, an assassin wouldn't think twice about killing the driver to keep them from contacting the police.

Fueled by fear for the innocent person Beau Daltrey might come across and use for his own selfish, criminal ends, Daisy sped up.

Crack!

She heard the sound of the gunshot behind her at the same time that pain seared her right thigh. She staggered forward and fell into a pile of busted-up wooden pallets. She'd dropped her gun. As she stretched out her right hand and grasped it, she heard footsteps coming up behind her.

Still lying on the ground, she whirled around and raised the pistol. Only to have a black-booted foot kick it out of her hand.

Beau Daltrey stood over her with a triumphant smile on his face and a pistol pointed at her head.

Behind him, back toward the street where the car chase had happened, she could see bits of flashing red and blue light. She could hear sirens. Law enforcement had arrived. But with all the noise that came with their arrival, they probably hadn't heard Daltrey fire his gun. Which meant help was not on the way.

"I could have shot and killed you as you jogged by," Daltrey said, his voice eerily emotionless and measured, as if he were giving a critique to a student. "But then I thought, I've earned the right to see your face when I pull the trigger. I've always looked forward to that. It's my favorite part of the job."

* * *

"Daisy!" Fear had such a stranglehold on Martin that he was surprised he could make a sound. He ran down the street, searching for her, knowing that she'd gone looking for Daltrey after Harry told him he and Leon had seen only two people in the mobster car when they'd approached it.

"Daisy!" Martin yelled again, desperate for her to hear him over the sounds of sirens and car engines and the blare of police radios.

He should have never left her side. He should never for a minute have thought that she'd stay in the truck. He *knew* her better than that.

He knew her and he loved her and what was happening right now was proof that he'd been an idiot for playing it safe, for keeping his distance. He'd been holding back from declaring his true feelings and pursuing a future together with Daisy because... Why? *Foolishness.* What he had with Daisy was precious. The love and the connection were real.

It didn't matter that he was clueless about how to make a real romantic partnership work. The whole idea that it was even possible for *anyone* to have things figured out ahead of time in such a dangerous and uncertain world was ridiculous. He and Daisy could make it through whatever it took to work things out, like they'd already done so many times before. So they could form their own strong and happy family.

They could do that if he hadn't already blown it with her.

What he'd grown up with didn't have to be his future. Words from a Bible verse formed in his mind. *I will even make a way in the wilderness.* Martin could lean into his faith for that pathway. Those weren't just frilly words. They pointed toward a practical solution.

All of his thoughts and feelings came together and focused on one single goal. He had to find Daisy alive. He couldn't bear the thought of losing her. And didn't want to spend another minute pretending they were *just friends* when they were so much more.

At least for him they were. How she felt after he'd spent so much time acting like an idiot was still an open question.

He stood on the sidewalk and spun around, looking for her. Had she actually seen Beau Daltrey and chased him? Or had she tried to guess which way he'd gone?

Trying to mimic the reasoning Daisy would have used was the only option he had. She would have gone toward the shadows and the darker side of the street. He headed in that direction, and as he got closer he saw the alleyway. That would be the fastest way for Daltrey to get out of sight. And that was probably the way Daisy went.

He ran into the alley. "Daisy!"

It was mostly filled with shadow, but in the small section of light several yards ahead he saw some kind of movement. He saw the flash of something swinging in an arc. It looked like a wooden plank. And then he heard the splintering sound of the wood connecting with something. Or someone.

Martin was already sprinting forward when he heard a gunshot and the *ping* of a bullet ricocheting off the asphalt.

Daisy! He could see her! She was on the ground, twisted to one side, a broken wooden plank in her hand.

Beau Daltrey was on his knees nearby, a fragment of the plank beside him where Daisy had apparently hit him. He was getting to his feet. Martin could see the assassin lifting a gun and aiming it toward Daisy at point-blank range.

Never one to quit, even facing impossible odds, Daisy reached for the gun right in front of her face.

At the same time Martin yelled, "No!"

Daltrey turned toward Martin. As Martin tackled him, Daisy knocked the gun out of Daltrey's hand and managed to clench her forearm across the hit man's neck, increasing the pressure and making it impossible for him to fight until Martin was able to land a knock-out blow.

Daltrey slumped to the ground. Martin quickly rolled him over so that he was facedown and slapped a set of cuffs on his wrists.

"Are you okay?" Martin asked Daisy as he slid his phone out of his pocket.

"I'm fine."

He got to his feet and called Harry. He told him where they were and what had happened, and then told him to send the cops. After he disconnected, he saw the blood soaking Daisy's jeans on her lower thigh near her knee. His heart nearly leaped out of his chest. "You've been shot."

"I think the bullet just grazed me," she said, still sitting on the ground. "But it does sting a bit."

Two cops ran down the alley toward them, with Harry and Leon alongside them. The first cop ran straight to Daltrey and made certain the hit man was secured. The second cop turned on a flashlight and quickly shined it around, likely making certain the scene was safe and there were no further threats.

Daisy slowly began pushing herself to her feet.

Martin reached for her arm to steady her. "Maybe you should just stay sitting until we can get a paramedic over here."

She shook her head. "No. It's not life-threatening. I can get to a clinic on my own and get it checked out." She stood and gestured toward Daltrey, who was moaning and starting to regain consciousness. "When he opens his eyes, I want him to see that he's in custody and I'm still standing."

"You are one tough woman," Martin said. He was feeling nearly giddy with relief and realized he was smiling despite the grim situation.

"You're pretty tough, too." Daisy mirrored his grin. "I think you might be getting the hang of this bounty hunter business." She nodded. "I've taught you well."

He laughed and it felt good. There weren't many things that lifted his spirits as much as being teased by Daisy.

More cops arrived in the alley. Daltrey regained consciousness and was arrested and walked out to a patrol car. As he passed by, he glanced in Daisy and Martin's direction, barely lifting his head. He looked defeated.

They walked side by side down the alley, back toward Martin's truck. It was still in the middle of the road, along with several cop cars. The mobster car was also still there, but it was empty now that the Miami mob couple had been arrested and driven away.

Daisy and Martin were going to be spending a lot of time talking with law enforcement tonight, giving their statements on the car chase and shootings, the attack in the alley and the murder of Ivan Bunker. That meant it would be a long time before the two of them were alone and Martin could tell Daisy all the things he wanted to say to her. Things that he should probably say in a setting much more romantic than a major crime scene in the middle of the night with icy drizzle still falling.

But the fact was Martin had already waited way too long. And he didn't want to wait a minute longer.

When they got to the sidewalk, he reached for her hand and stopped. Daisy stopped alongside him, and they turned to face each other. Martin looked into those big brown eyes of hers, so full of spirit and honesty, and a little bit of fire. Even after all she'd been through, there was still that spark that made her so fascinating and, yes, challenging at times. He sighed and smiled, thinking of the little things about her that drove him crazy. And he wouldn't have it any other way.

"Just before I found you here in the alley, I was afraid I'd lost you," he said.

She made a scoffing sound. "It's not that easy to get rid of me."

"Yeah, well, you're about to realize that it's not that easy to get rid of me, either," Martin said. His throat was beginning to burn a little. Maybe it was the icy weather. Maybe it was emotion. He cleared it and started again. "I love you, Daisy Lopez. I've loved you for a long time." He shook his head. "I don't want to dig into the past and try to explain what I was thinking or what I was doing. Other than to tell you that I was afraid that if you and I got too close, I'd mess everything up."

He reached for her other hand, so that he was now holding both of them. "I think we've wasted too much time. And I hope you haven't given up on me."

Daisy raised her eyebrows and lifted her chin, and Martin found himself laughing nervously because he knew from experience that that look meant she was getting ready to tease and torment him a little bit.

But then her dark eyes began to fill with unshed tears. "I've tried to give up on you," she said. "But it never would stick." She sniffed loudly and a couple of fat tears rolled down her cheeks. "I love you, too."

Martin leaned toward her and pressed his lips to hers. The kiss, soft and warm, felt every bit as good as he'd ever imagined. He let go of her hands and slid his own hands toward the small of her back, drawing her closer to him. Holding her in his arms, he felt as if he'd gotten everything he'd ever wanted. As if every dream he'd ever had was finally coming true. As if he finally had the home he'd always longed for.

Slowly and reluctantly, they broke off the kiss and each of them took a small step back.

"Will you marry me?" Martin asked, the words coming straight from his heart and out of his mouth as easy as breathing.

"Yes," Daisy nodded, grinning broadly. "I believe I will."

EPILOGUE

One month later

"Your dad would be so proud of you." Shannon Lopez beamed at her daughter.

Daisy smiled in return, feeling like she was beaming, too. Warm, sunny happiness flowed through her as she leaned into Martin, *her husband*, who'd wrapped his arm around her shoulder and now held her close to his side.

"I think Joe would be proud of you, too," she said to Martin. "He only knew you for a short time before the accident took him, but he liked you. He would have appreciated what you've done with your life. And I know he would have been happy to see you and Daisy fall in love."

Daisy glanced at Martin and saw the hopefulness and vulnerability in his eyes. She knew it was hard for him to open his heart, and to deal with the fragile uncertainty of a heartfelt moment without making a joke to create some distance.

"Thank you," he said, his voice husky with emotion. "That means a lot to me."

His own parents had not shown up for the small

wedding ceremony at the church earlier this afternoon. Whether they would show up for this relaxed, open house–style reception at the Peak Bail Bonds office remained to be seen. There was nothing he and Daisy could do about the family dynamic that Martin was born into. But they could do a lot about the life they lived now and the future as they fashioned their own family.

Martin's Rock Solid Bail Bonds family had shown up for both the wedding and the reception, and from what Daisy could tell that had been enough to make Martin happy. And that made her happy.

"If you lovebirds would scoot over a bit we could slide this couch over here." Ramona Orlansky, wife of bounty hunter Harry Orlansky, smiled broadly at Daisy. Ramona worked at her family's diner in Stone River and she'd graciously brought a selection of homemade pies to be served in lieu of wedding cake. To say the pies were a hit with the guests and the wedding party was an understatement.

Daisy and Martin stepped out of the way. They had wanted to get married as soon as possible rather than scheduling a fancy wedding several months into the future. They figured they'd already waited long enough to be together. Millie had offered the use of the first floor of the Peak Bail Bonds office for their reception, and after discussing it for a few minutes, Daisy and Martin had come to the conclusion that it would be perfect. They just hadn't counted on so many people wanting to stop by late on a snowy afternoon to offer their congratulations, so extra chairs and couches had needed to be brought down from the upstairs apartments.

Shannon gave Daisy a quick kiss on the cheek before walking toward Millie and Alvis, who were already chatting with Sheriff Russell and her husband. Daisy and Martin stepped out of the way so Ramona and Harry could slide the couch into place.

"I suppose we should mingle with our guests," Martin said to Daisy.

That would be a little bit hard to do. Daisy looked around at the packed office. Despite the humble potluck-style food offerings—other than the towering whipped cream–covered pies that did not look at all humble—everybody who had dropped by seemed to want to stay for a while.

The sounds of laughter and easy conversation swirled around them. As did the scents of tacos and enchiladas and fresh salsa.

Daisy's stomach growled.

"Why don't you two sit down," Ramona said. "This is supposed to be your day. Harry and I will go get you something to eat."

"And while we're at it, we can get ourselves something to eat, too," Harry said to his wife as they walked away, wrapping an arm around her waist as they went.

Daisy sat on the sofa and Martin sat beside her. Daisy's pearl-white dress was ankle length with an off-the-shoulder neckline. She looked at her matching pumps with spiked heels. There was no way she could chase down a bad guy in those. She turned to her brand-new husband, who wore a dark gray suit, a tie the same pearl-white color as Daisy's dress, and cowboy boots.

Martin took her hand and squeezed it. She gazed into his eyes and thought about how much she looked forward to being with him for the rest of her life.

"Here, Harry said to give these to you and to tell you your food would be here in a minute." Cassie Wheeler, Martin's boss at Rock Solid Bail Bonds, had carried glasses of fruit punch and handed them over to Daisy and Martin.

Leon Bragg, who was also her employee, stood beside her holding punch for the two of them. As soon as Cassie's hands were empty, he handed her a glass and they both sat down in chairs that faced the couch. It seemed to Daisy like nearly every time she saw the stylish, strawberry blonde bail bondswoman, the big bounty hunter was nearby.

"So," Cassie began, "things have been so hectic for the last month that I haven't had time to get caught up with everything. I know that you got paid the recovery fee for capturing Beau Daltrey since you did actually apprehend him before the cops did. Congratulations."

"Thanks," Daisy said. She exchanged a smile with Martin.

"What happened to everybody else involved in the case?" Cassie asked. "What did you learn after everything was wrapped up?"

"Well, Beau Daltrey was sent back to Miami to face his original murder charges," Daisy said. "At some point he'll face charges for all the things he did while he was here in Montana. His fellow mobsters who came to Jameson, including the one who shot and killed Ivan Bunker, are all locked up and facing charges, as well."

Millie had drifted over and Cassie glanced at her. "I can't imagine how it felt to find out your own employee, Justine, was secretly working against you."

"Justine and Robbie have a lot to answer for, including the fact that Robbie was selling drugs with Tony Valens." Millie sighed. "Apparently, when Daltrey and Bunker first hit town, before Daisy got the case and started hunting for them, they thought they might stay awhile. They needed a source of income, and they decided that since they'd seen drug dealing in the mob they could do that. They went to the university campus assuming they'd find people buying and selling drugs who'd be willing to work with them. Unfortunately, they were right.

"I let the prosecutors know that Justine and Robbie gave us information that helped Daisy and Martin capture the bad guys. Justine is not in touch with us anymore, so I don't know what will happen to them. But I wish them the best."

"What do you know about the Miami mob side of everything?" Leon asked Daisy.

"The informant inside the mob said the criminal bosses had had enough of the whole thing. They never authorized Daltrey and Bunker to skip bail to begin with. Their orders were to keep their mouths shut, not rat anybody out and do their time in prison if the mob lawyer couldn't prevent a conviction."

"So the mob wasn't particularly in a hurry to help them get out of Jameson."

"Right. They were also mad about the unauthorized drug business. They did send their decoys to distract law enforcement, just as we thought. But the couple was actually an assassin team sent to kill both Bunker and Daltrey. But they didn't intend to kill Daltrey until after he'd helped them locate me. Of course, Daltrey didn't know that. They lied and told him they had to kill Bunker because Bunker was secretly feeding me information on the fugitives' whereabouts."

Daisy blew out a deep breath. Surviving that ordeal had been exhausting. And terrifying. Martin squeezed her hand. "There's nothing quite like the reminder that we aren't here forever to help you get your priorities straight," he said to her quietly.

And to encourage a person to face some of their deepest fears, Daisy thought.

"So we won't need to keep an eye out for the mob when you move to Stone River?" Cassie asked.

Millie and Alvis had decided that now was a good time for them to retire. Daisy and Martin were planning to stay in Jameson to help them wrap things up. After that, they'd move to Stone River, where Daisy would be joining the Rock Solid team.

"No," Daisy said. "You won't."

Martin leaned in close to Daisy. "We have an appointment to keep," he said, his breath tickling her neck and warming her cheeks. "And it's just about time." He stood and extended his hand to her. She took it and rose to her feet. "Excuse us," he said to everyone who was sitting near them. "We'll be back in just a few minutes."

Martin led the way to the tiny room that served as the office's break room and kitchen. Once he and Daisy were inside, they closed the door behind them.

"I'm so glad you thought of this," Daisy said.

Martin had always had a thoughtful side, even when they were *just friends*. And she had recently learned he had quite the sentimental side, too.

Her husband slid his phone out of his pocket and started tapping the screen. "If I planned this right, it is now nine in the morning in Guam," Martin said. "And if I didn't? Oh, well."

Daisy pressed her hands together, feeling like a child bursting to tell a secret. But this wasn't a secret. It was a promise being kept.

The phone rang a couple of times on the other side of the world, and then Aaron Lopez's face appeared on the screen. "Hey," he said. "So, does this mean it's official and I have a brother-in-law?"

"Yes!" Daisy said. "We're here at the office celebrating with Mom and some friends. But you are the very first person we've called as husband and wife." She'd been smiling all afternoon and here she was smiling again. "It seemed right to make a special call to you since you were the one who brought Martin and me together all those years ago."

"I love you, sis, and I'm happy for you," Aaron said. "And I'm glad the friend who is as close as a brother is now officially my brother."

"I'm just sorry it took so long," Martin said.

On the screen, Aaron laughed. "Oh, I imagine it took exactly the amount of time it was supposed to take. Welcome to the family, Martin. You two take care of each other."

Daisy and Martin smiled at one another. "We will," they answered together.

* * * * *

Dear Reader,

I hope you had fun riding along with Daisy and Martin as they unraveled their feelings for one another while chasing bad guys and trying to not get killed in the process. In the end, Daisy captures her fugitives—plus some extra criminals—and earns her bounty hunter fee. And Martin, while working alongside her, realizes he doesn't have to be locked into his past. He can learn from life experiences and press on in faith toward the life and love he truly wants. Even if, at the moment, he isn't sure exactly where he's going or how he'll get there. The same is true for all of us. We can press on in faith, even if we aren't certain of every step to take on the road ahead. What a relief!

Thank you for taking the time to read *Hostage Pursuit*. I'll be checking in with bail bondswoman Cassie Wheeler and her bounty hunting team in the upcoming third Rock Solid Bounty Hunters romance. I'm sure there'll be something exciting going on. There always is with this crew. For some reason they actually like to go looking for trouble.

I love to hear from my readers. If you're inclined to write, my email address is Jenna@jennanight.com. I also have a Jenna Night Facebook page. You can sign up for my newsletter to be alerted to new book releases on my website, JennaNight.com. You can also follow me on BookBub.

Jenna

Get 4 FREE REWARDS!

We'll send you 2 FREE Books plus 2 FREE Mystery Gifts.

Love Inspired Suspense books showcase how courage and optimism unite in stories of faith and love in the face of danger.

FREE Value Over $20

YES! Please send me 2 FREE Love Inspired Suspense novels and my 2 FREE mystery gifts (gifts are worth about $10 retail). After receiving them, if I don't wish to receive any more books, I can return the shipping statement marked "cancel." If I don't cancel, I will receive 6 brand-new novels every month and be billed just $5.24 each for the regular-print edition or $5.99 each for the larger-print edition in the U.S., or $5.74 each for the regular-print edition or $6.24 each for the larger-print edition in Canada. That's a savings of at least 13% off the cover price. It's quite a bargain! Shipping and handling is just 50¢ per book in the U.S. and $1.25 per book in Canada.* I understand that accepting the 2 free books and gifts places me under no obligation to buy anything. I can always return a shipment and cancel at any time. The free books and gifts are mine to keep no matter what I decide.

Choose one: ☐ **Love Inspired Suspense Regular-Print** (153/353 IDN GNWN) ☐ **Love Inspired Suspense Larger-Print** (107/307 IDN GNWN)

Name (please print)

Address   Apt. #

City   State/Province   Zip/Postal Code

Email: Please check this box ☐ if you would like to receive newsletters and promotional emails from Harlequin Enterprises ULC and its affiliates. You can unsubscribe anytime.

Mail to the **Reader Service:**
IN U.S.A.: P.O. Box 1341, Buffalo, NY 14240-8531
IN CANADA: P.O. Box 603, Fort Erie, Ontario L2A 5X3

Want to try 2 free books from another series? Call 1-800-873-8635 or visit www.ReaderService.com.

*Terms and prices subject to change without notice. Prices do not include sales taxes, which will be charged (if applicable) based on your state or country of residence. Canadian residents will be charged applicable taxes. Offer not valid in Quebec. This offer is limited to one order per household. Books received may not be as shown. Not valid for current subscribers to Love Inspired Suspense books. All orders subject to approval. Credit or debit balances in a customer's account(s) may be offset by any other outstanding balance owed by or to the customer. Please allow 4 to 6 weeks for delivery. Offer available while quantities last.

Your Privacy—Your information is being collected by Harlequin Enterprises ULC, operating as Reader Service. For a complete summary of the information we collect, how we use this information and to whom it is disclosed, please visit our privacy notice located at corporate.harlequin.com/privacy-notice. From time to time we may also exchange your personal information with reputable third parties. If you wish to opt out of this sharing of your personal information, please visit readerservice.com/consumerschoice or call 1-800-873-8635. **Notice to California Residents**—Under California law, you have specific rights to control and access your data. For more information on these rights and how to exercise them, visit corporate.harlequin.com/california-privacy.

LIS20R2

After another bullet whizzed by, Autumn turned, trying
to get a better view of the gunman. She had to figure out
where he was.

"Stay behind the tree," she whispered to Derek. "And
keep an eye on Sherlock."

Finally, she spotted a gunman crouched behind a
nearby boulder. The front of his Glock was pointed at her.

A Glock? The man definitely wasn't a hunter.

Autumn already knew that, though.

Hunters didn't aim their guns at people.

Her gaze continued to scan the area. She spotted
another man behind a tree and a third man behind another
boulder.

Who were these guys? And what did they want from
Autumn?

Backup couldn't get here soon enough.

The breeze picked up again, bringing another smattering of rain with it. They didn't have much time here. The conditions were going to become perilous at any minute. The storm might drive the gunman away, but it would present other dangers in the process.

She spotted a fourth man behind another tree in the distance. They all surrounded the campsite where Derek and his brother had set up.

They'd been waiting for Derek to return, hadn't they?

Why? What sense did that make?

She didn't have time to think about that now. Another bullet came flying past, piercing a nearby tree.

"What are we going to do?" Derek whispered. "Can I help?"

"Just stay behind a tree and remain quiet," she said. "We don't want to make this too easy for them."

Sherlock let out a little whine, but Autumn shushed the dog.

The man fired again. This time the bullet split the wood only inches from her.

Autumn's heart raced. These men were out for blood.

Even if the men ran out of bullets, she and Derek were going to be outnumbered. They couldn't just wait here for that to happen.

She had to act—and now.

She turned, pulling her gun's trigger.

Don't miss
Mountain Survival *by Christy Barritt,*
available March 2021 wherever Love Inspired Suspense
books and ebooks are sold.

LoveInspired.com

LOVE INSPIRED
INSPIRATIONAL ROMANCE

UPLIFTING STORIES OF FAITH, FORGIVENESS AND HOPE.

Join our social communities to connect with other readers who share your love!

Sign up for the Love Inspired newsletter at **LoveInspired.com** to be the first to find out about upcoming titles, special promotions and exclusive content.

CONNECT WITH US AT:

Facebook.com/LoveInspiredBooks

Twitter.com/LoveInspiredBks

Facebook.com/groups/HarlequinConnection

LISOCIAL2020

HARLEQUIN

Heartfelt or thrilling, passionate or uplifting—Harlequin is more than just happily-ever-after.

With twelve different series to choose from and new books available every month, you are sure to find stories that will move you, uplift you, inspire and delight you.

SIGN UP FOR THE HARLEQUIN NEWSLETTER

Be the first to hear about great new reads and exciting offers!

Harlequin.com/newsletters